INCEPTION
THE GENESIS MACHINE
BOOK 1

K. J. GILLENWATER

This is a work of fiction. Names, characters, places, and incidents are products of the author's imagination or are used fictitiously and are not to be construed as real. Any resemblance to actual events, locales, organizations, or persons, living or dead, is entirely coincidental.

Inception

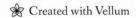 Created with Vellum

CHAPTER 1

July 2022
Fort Madison, Iowa

PETTY OFFICER RYAN LEDBETTER stepped through the
rising waters outside the secure perimeter of the
NAVSECGRU detachment headquarters on Fort Madison.
Rain pummeled him and ran off his raincoat in sheets. His
watch cap was soaked through.

"This is bullshit. We should be following evac procedures."
He shone his flashlight through the murky dark, and it bounced
off the chain link fence which surrounded the compound.
"There's nothing out here. Rounds are done." He snapped off
his flashlight and headed for the gates. He'd be damned if he'd
wade through rounds the rest of his twelve hour shift. The
commander should've let them leave hours ago.

"Wait." Seaman Bradley Conlon, his watch partner, stood
still. "Do you hear that?"

Newbies always took this watch shit too seriously. "There's

nothing there, Conlon. Come on, let's go back inside." His flash-light flickered out. He shook it. The light wavered. "Dammit."

A tremendous roar filled his ears. Like a tornado. A shrieking blast of sound. Instinctually, he covered them to protect himself from the noise. His whole body shook with the force of it.

Conlon was yelling something at him. He pointed at the sky.

Ledbetter looked up. Overhead, less than twenty feet above them, a huge ball of fire streaked by.

The object lost altitude rapidly and headed toward the swollen Mississippi, which edged the base. It slammed into the shallows sending flames and chunks of debris everywhere. Within minutes, the fire was doused by the flood waters and rain.

Ledbetter pressed the button on his walkie talkie. "This is Petty Officer Ledbetter. I think a plane crashed. We need emergency vehicles on site ASAP." He ran toward the rubble even before he was done speaking. "Come on Conlon. There might be survivors."

Conlon held back. "That was no plane."

Ledbetter turned and slowed his run through the mushy, flooded grass. "What do you mean?"

"It was just a big ball. There weren't any wings, no tail." Conlon splashed down the slope to him. "Let's go check it out."

Through the sheet-like rain they slipped and slid their way down the riverbank. Visibility was practically nil. Ledbetter shook his flashlight once more. It popped on. He played the white light across the grassy shoreline, now under a foot of water and rising. The beam caught a jagged edge of something sticking up from the ground.

"Over here." Ledbetter headed for the strange thing only a

few yards away. The water came up over his chukka boots, wetting his wool socks. He paid it no mind. The object in the shallow water grabbed his attention.

A blob, about eight feet across and cracked open like a nut, sat in front of him. Smoke rose from the center, and the whole thing hissed in the rain and damp. He reached out to touch one jagged edge. His fingers hit something spongy and slimy. Like snot. "What the hell?" He yanked back his hand and wiped it on his dungarees. A chill ran through him.

Conlon stood right behind him. "What is it?" He reached out to touch it, too, but Ledbetter stopped him.

"Don't. I don't know what the hell that thing is, but it ain't no plane, and it ain't no meteor." Ledbetter picked up his radio once more and pushed the talk button. "This is Ledbetter again. I think you need to get someone down here."

CHAPTER 2

Defense Language Institute, Monterey, CA
August 2023

CHARLIE CUTTER SLICED into the water, her arms in perfect rhythm. The silence under water soothed her as she focused on her freestyle stroke—her routine four times a week. Her mind clear, her breathing timed.

One, two, three. Breathe. One, two, three. Breathe.

Swimming was one of two things she'd been naturally gifted at from an early age.

Two more laps, and she'd be done with her two thousand meters.

She hit the end of the pool, prepared to flip, but a hand touched her arm.

She came up out of the water with a gasp. Concentration broken. The quiet calm of her routine interrupted.

"Petty Officer Cutter?" A pimply-faced seaman in his summer whites crouched down at the edge of the pool.

Charlie looked past him at the clock on the wall. She'd been on her best time. Dammit. "Could you hand me that?" She nodded at her plain white towel sitting on a bench near the women's locker room door.

The seaman's face reddened, but he did what she asked.

Newbies, like this one, who waited for a new cycle of language classes to start, pulled odd assignments to fill in the empty days. A linguist-in-training at the Defense Language Institute might wait months for his spot in class, which meant he spent every day 'on duty.' Only the lucky ones got plum assignments. Looked like this poor seaman, bewildered and nervous, must've gotten a crap job of some kind.

Charlie climbed out of the pool, adjusted her racing suit, and wrapped the thin towel around her. "What can I do for you, Hansen?" She read the nametag pinned crookedly to his pressed white cotton shirt. He'd been lucky there'd been no surprise uniform inspection this morning at muster. The Petty Officer-in-Charge would've noticed that.

"Commander Niels wanted me to find you. Your roommate told me you'd be here at the gym." He cleared his throat. "I didn't know you'd be in the pool."

Was it her fault the kid had probably never been this close to a woman in a swimsuit before? She was surprised he'd made it through the rigors of Boot Camp with his spindly arms and nervous jack rabbit twitches. "Lieutenant Commander Niels?" She'd met him once, the day after she'd arrived in Monterey. He'd been a classmate of her father's. Even from three thousand miles away, Captain Harrison Cutter kept tabs on her.

"Something about your orders?" Hansen stood at parade rest, a horrible habit leftover from training. It took a few months for most to lose such an obvious newbie trademark. "I have a van parked out front. I'll wait for you there."

She dried her hair with the towel. "Give me five."

———

Charlie, her hair braided but dripping under her cover, shivered in the passenger van. Although it was mid-August, air conditioning was unneeded in the mild Central Coast climate. She gave Hansen the evil eye from the bench seat behind him, but he kept his gaze focused on the winding road.

"So tell me, how hard is it?" Hansen stopped at the bottom of the hill and sneaked a glance at her in the mirror. "Class, I mean."

"What are you taking?" DLI offered every language under the sun. She'd even run into a few civvies from the FBI here to take a Tagalog course once.

"Persian-Farsi."

"My roommate's taking that. Not bad, she says. Do you know French?"

"No."

"Well, I've heard it's similar to French. I'm sure you'll be fine. Forty-seven weeks, just like Russian, and I survived."

"Yeah, but you're—" He broke eye contact with her and made the turn toward the administration buildings. "—different."

Her heart seized up. She'd heard that before. Languages came naturally to her, maybe a little too naturally. Her teachers, little old ladies from the Ukraine and Russia, had suspected she'd studied Russian before. She hadn't. "Don't worry, Hansen. You'll be fine. It takes a lot to rock out."

"Guess I'll find out in September."

Charlie nodded. Most students did well at DLI. But most of them studied their hearts out. Flashcards with vocab, doing assignments for hours in their heavy workbooks, listening to the foreign news stations. For her, that was all a waste of time. Her brain latched onto language like a wolverine did its prey. Russian had been a bit more of a challenge with its four declensions, however. After a few weeks she'd gobbled down the grammar rules so quickly, her instructors kept her busy with new vocabulary while teaching the rest of her class. Most expected her to pass her Defense Language Proficiency Test, or DLPT, with an across the board four-rating on a five point scale. Almost impossible for someone new to the language.

"Here we are." Hansen parked outside the two-story cement block building that served as the Navy administration headquarters for the language students.

"Thanks. Good luck in class." She stepped out of the van and made sure her cover sat level on her head and her white cotton uniform skirt was wrinkle free. The commander of the naval detachment would notice those details. The last thing she wanted was Lieutenant Commander Niels reporting to her father about her less-than-perfect appearance.

When she walked inside, a young admin sat behind a desk. By the hashes on the sleeve of her uniform, Charlie could see she was an E-5, Petty Officer Second Class.

"I'm here to see Lieutenant Commander Niels." Charlie took off her cover. The inside brim was damp from her hair. A slight chill ran through her. She'd been a good student, never been in trouble, and did well on her physical fitness tests. Had her father decided to meddle again?

The E-5 pressed a few buttons on her phone and talked quietly into the receiver. "The Lieutenant Commander wants me to send you up."

Charlie headed for the stairwell. She was so close to finishing her class—of course her father would intervene and make a mess of things. Calling in a favor, probably. He couldn't sign her up for Officer Candidate School without her permission, could he?

She headed right for the commander's door, a wooden placard with his name painted in gold lettering next to a ship's wheel. She knocked.

"Come."

She took a deep breath and opened the door.

Lieutenant Commander Niels had ruddy cheeks and a halo of gray hair around a shiny bald crown. "Petty Officer Cutter, have a seat, please."

Charlie stood stiffly in front of his desk. She had to know. She couldn't wait for him to explain the point of her visit. "Sir, I want to be a linguist. I wouldn't have joined if I didn't. If my father thinks that I'd give that up to please him, well—"

Niels cracked a smile. "Please, have a seat, Cutter. Your father didn't have anything to do with this meeting."

When she heard those words, she lost her train of thought. Why else would he ask her here? She sat in the hard metal seat with a blue fabric cushion—standard Navy issue.

Niels settled back in his chair. "It's come to my attention your skills would be better suited to a different assignment than your original orders. I've never seen this type of request come across my desk. Instead of heading to Goodfellow in Texas after graduation, you've been reassigned to the Naval Criminal Investigative Services."

"What?"

He raised an eyebrow.

"I'm sorry, sir, but I don't understand. I have orders to Japan —Misawa. I want to be airborne. That's why I joined." Did her father have something to do with this unprecedented shift in plans despite what the commander said? He'd never liked the idea of his daughter being enlisted much less riding in a spy plane gathering enemy comms. "If Captain Cutter gave you some idea that I'm unhappy here—"

"I told you, Cutter, I haven't spoken with your father. In fact, I'm rather insulted you'd believe that as commander of the naval detachment here at DLI I wouldn't have any say over the students in my purview. Or that I'd listen to a suggestion from an old Academy friend. That's not how things work in the Navy." Lieutenant Commander Niels's eyes snapped with fire, and his once smiling mouth turned down in a frown.

"No, sir."

"Good. Now, let me continue. You have new orders. After you've finished class, you will be headed directly to the Washington Navy Yard and will check in there to find out more about your assignment."

"Yes, sir."

"Do you have any questions?"

A million questions ran through her head, but most of them not ones she'd ask the Lieutenant Commander. "They want a CTI straight from school with no equipment training? Why me?"

"The request came directly from the head of BUPERS. As I said, I've never had a request like this before, but you're an exceptional student, Cutter. This is a great opportunity for you." He handed her a manila envelope with her name scribbled across the front in black marker. "I wish you luck, sailor."

"Thank you, sir." She took the envelope.

"Take that with you and hand it to the Officer-in-Charge. Your PCS orders will be ready with the rest of your classmates' after graduation."

He stood up. Her cue to leave. "Yes, sir."

Once she'd left his office, her mind raced. Her father had to be wrapped up in this somehow because it didn't make any sense. She was nobody. A brand new E-4 fresh from language training. What could she possibly have that NCIS would want? Besides wasn't their mission internal? They investigated crimes within the Navy and the Marines. It didn't make sense.

The envelope grew heavy in her hands. No matter who'd been behind this switch, she was upset. Everything had been perfect. She was supposed to take her final language exam, transfer to Goodfellow Air Force Base in San Angelo for equipment training, and then flight school, followed by her final orders to Japan flying recon out of Misawa.

She wasn't a desk jockey.

She strode past the admin's desk and headed out the door, popping her cover back on her head. Hansen waited for her in the van, its engine running while parked next to the curb. She strolled right past him.

From her skirt pocket she plucked her cell phone. She chose a number out of her contact list and, while she waited for an answer on the other end, headed straight for the barracks up the hill.

"Cutter here," a gruff voice rumbled in her ear.

"What did you do?" She could hear the strained anger in her own words. The accusations she wanted to let fly. But she was determined to keep a cool head this time. Show him she could act the grown up and not like the typical teenager he still liked to compare her to. "Why did you have them change my orders?"

"Charlene, what are you talking about? Where are you?"

Why did he call her that? He knew she hated it. "You know very well where I am. You're screwing with my life again. Why don't you just admit it?"

He sighed. "I'd love to say I have been. Trust me, I've been chomping at the bit to get you out of there—but I swear to you, I've kept my word."

He sounded sincere. Charlie, her pace so quick she was out of breath, stopped in mid-stride. "You swear?"

"Yes."

Silence settled. Charlie's mind raced. "Then I don't understand." If her father wasn't involved in all of this, what was going on?

"You say you received new orders?"

"Yes. To some place called—" She opened up the manila envelope. "—NCIS-A Division. Do you know what that is?" Her father had been in the Navy her whole life. Captain Harrison Cutter was a well-respected intelligence analyst at the National Security Agency. She might butt heads with him frequently, but occasionally he was good for a few things.

"No. But why would they want you? That's police work. You're only a linguistics major."

The usual dig at her choice in college majors. She reined in her temper as best she could and let the slight roll off her back. "Look, I was hoping you might have been responsible for this, that's all. But since you clearly don't believe I'm qualified for the job in the first place, I guess I can throw that idea out the window. Say hi to Chad for me when you see him."

"Charlene, I didn't mean—"

Charlie hung up. He had a way of cutting her down every time she talked to him. Nothing was ever good enough for him. The last thing she needed to hear was his typical lecture about how she'd failed his expectations and why she made a huge mistake enlisting in the Navy rather than going to OCS.

She needed to burn off some of her anxious energy. A few more laps in the pool would do it. Her roommate thought she worked out too much, too hard, but it was one way for her to clear her head and forget about her dad's disappointments in her life choices.

There had to be a way out of this. If her father hadn't been the one behind it, she'd figure out who was. Damned if some idiot from NCIS would be telling her what to do. They'd already changed her orders once. There must be a way to change them again.

CHAPTER 3

CHARLIE SAT in the security lobby of Building forty-two—a nondescript, blocky structure. She needed a good swim to shake off her nerves. After working for months to perfect her language skills and be the best damned Russian linguist the Navy had, she found herself at the Washington Navy Yard surrounded by a bunch of civilians and contractors.

As she waited for her security badge and an escort to lead her to her new office and a job she knew nothing about, she stifled a yawn.

Last night she'd arrived at Reagan National with her duffle bag and a phone number scribbled on the back of her manila envelope—her sponsor. She'd dialed the number. No one answered. After waiting a half hour for someone to call her back, she'd given up, flagged down a taxi, and wandered around base with her overloaded bag and a wheeled carry-on looking for the Navy barracks.

"Petty Officer Cutter?"

Charlie looked up from the outdated magazine she'd been reading to see a tall, thin woman with chin-length curly hair standing in front of her. "Yes?"

At the same time, the security officer behind the desk called out her name, "Cutter. Your badge is ready." He held a laminated badge with her picture and a metal clip.

The woman in front of her smiled. "I'm Petty Officer Storm. Call me Lisa, please."

Charlie eyed her sleek tan trousers and bright blue short-sleeved sweater. "Where's your uniform?"

"Why don't you go grab your badge, and I'll explain everything on the way to the office."

A Navy assignment, a petty officer, and no uniform? This was growing more interesting.

Charlie rose from the couch and collected her badge from the man behind the counter, signing her name into the log.

"If you ever forget your badge," the man told her, "you need to stop in here to pick up a temporary badge for the day. If you lose your badge, make sure to contact base security immediately. Your badge is your responsibility. If it does end up lost or stolen, don't expect a slap on the wrist."

Charlie nodded and clipped it to the pocket of her uniform shirt.

"Let's go." Lisa stood at the door, holding it open for her. "Commander Orr is waiting for you. We've got a lot to cover in a short period of time to make sure you're up to speed."

Charlie stepped out of the security office. Wow, the foot traffic had picked up considerably since she'd arrived at 0730. Beyond the lobby and the security office, stood a row of turnstiles. Each was equipped with a separate slot and a red/green light. A soldier in camo stepped up to an empty turnstile, pulled his security badge down from its retractable line around his neck, and slid it into the slot. When he pulled it free, the light turned from red to green, and he pushed through the turnstile. Behind him another worker lined up for the same process.

Lisa stepped in line behind a few others and signaled Charlie to follow her. As they waited their turn, Lisa gave her some instructions. "Don't pull your card out too quickly, or you might cause an error. Too many errors in a row, and you'll be locked out."

"Locked out?"

"Just means you'll have to make a stop at the security office and have them straighten you out. But I'm sure you can tell they don't like mistakes in there."

The man's speech about losing her badge and what that might mean still rung in her ears. Before she could ask any more questions, Lisa was sliding her card into the slot. The turnstile clicked, and she pushed through to the other side.

Charlie stepped up for her turn. Since she only had her badge clipped to her pocket, unlike everyone else who had it attached to a retractable line, she had to unclip it to put it into the reader. She slid it in and out, taking her time. The light stayed red. Her palms began to sweat. It wouldn't do on her first day of work to make mistakes. She didn't want to go back into that security office and explain that the reader wouldn't accept her card.

Lisa held up her own security pass and turned it around. "You put it in backwards. It has to go in like this." She showed her how the card had to be put in the slot with the magnetic strip facing away from her.

Relief shot through her. The line was building behind her, so the pressure was on. Quickly, she re-entered her card the correct way, and the green light came on.

Charlie caught up to her new co-worker.

Thank goodness she'd made it through.

To the right several people entered codes into keypads that

lined the walls. A big metal drawer popped open for one person.

"What's that?" she asked.

"That's where we collect our office key every morning. Well, that's where Commander Orr gets it from. He has to pick it up and drop it off every day. Lieutenant Kellerman also knows the combination in case it's needed."

"But we're inside a secure facility. Why would they need a key?" Charlie thought her clearance would give her all the access she needed.

Lisa smiled and led her down the hall toward a bank of elevators. "There are multiple levels of security here. We work with compartmented information. Each office has its own secrets. You'll see. I can't tell you much more about it here." Lisa nodded at the stream of workers headed toward their respective offices.

Thousands of people worked in this building. She'd watched them pass by while she waited in the security office. The layers of cars parked outside revealed a lot more went on inside the building than she'd realized. With only a few floors visible from the street, she wondered where they all disappeared to.

Charlie and Lisa hopped into an elevator. A half-dozen military and civilian personnel got inside with them. There was a row of buttons. Only a third of them were marked. One through seven were clear as day. Then, beneath were the unmarked buttons. The arrow above the door indicated they were going down.

After a few people pressed some of the unmarked buttons, Lisa reached forward and pressed the button on the bottom of the left column. "That's our floor. Don't forget it."

Charlie nodded. She wished someone would tell her more

about who she was working for, why they'd chosen her, but Lisa had made it clear they couldn't talk about much here in the open. Even amidst all of these other military and government workers with security clearances as high as hers. She kept her mouth shut.

The elevator slowly emptied out. People trickled out in bits and pieces as they descended down further and further. Eventually, it was only the two of them and one lone Marine. The elevator slowed. The last floor. Theirs.

"Follow me." Lisa led her to the left. A series of doors on either side of the hallway greeted her. Each one had a keypad and a slot on the wall next to the doorknob. There were several shorter hallways leading off the main one with signs indicating room numbers in each wing. Lisa made another left down another hallway. The door at the very end of the hall was marked 1271. Lisa slid her security badge into the slot and pressed some numbers. The door clicked.

"I'll give you the code once we're inside the office. Memorize it. Never share it with anyone. It changes every six months. Hope you have a good head for numbers." Lisa turned the knob and opened the door.

————

The office behind the door looked like any other office. Cubicles. Computers. A stained coffeemaker next to the printer.

"Welcome to NCIS-A Division." Lisa led her down a short row of cubicles. "Chief, Petty Officer Cutter is here. This is Chief Ricard."

In the last cubicle at the end of the row a face popped out. He leaned back in his chair to take a good look at who was headed his way. Chief Ricard, red-faced and round-cheeked with a receding hairline, gave her a wink. "Cutter." He smiled. "Good to have you join us. Stormy, I can take it from here. Why don't you grab our new team member a cup of java." He stabbed a chubby finger in her direction. "Cream? Sugar? How do you like it?"

"Black is fine." The coffee had smelled burned to her when she entered the office, but no one could be in the military without a heavy coffee addiction. Burned or no.

"My kinda gal. You're all right, Cutter." He spun his chair around to face her head on. Unlike Lisa or 'Stormy,' he wore his tan chief's uniform. She needed to find out what kind of dress was required here. "Have a seat. We'll show you to your cube in a sec." He rested his hands on his ample stomach, which was barely within regulation weight, she guessed.

Charlie grabbed an empty chair and rolled it out into the aisle. She set her cover and her purse on the desk behind her.

Chief Ricard snatched a folder off his desk and opened it. "Petty Officer Charlene Cutter. Language school. Top of her class, it says. Pretty impressive PT scores as well."

"I prefer to be called Charlie."

He shifted his gaze to her face. "Cutter. We go by last names around here."

"Right." Although the chief appeared about as harmless as a teddy bear, he clearly had a tough interior.

He focused back on her folder. "I'll bet you're wondering how you pulled this assignment."

Her heart thumped. "Yes. The Commandant back at DLI didn't give me much to work with. I thought I was all set for Misawa." The disappointment still burned inside her. Now instead of flying with recon planes over the Kamchatka Penin- sula, she was sitting in a room with no windows, one door, and a dozen cubicles. Not exactly the exciting military career she'd envisioned when she signed up.

"The Commander wants to brief you in detail once he arrives. He had an early meeting this morning upstairs. But I'm supposed to settle you in, introduce you to the rest of the group, make sure you're set up. That kind of thing." He thumbed through her papers.

"I understand, Chief." She hadn't seen where the 'rest of the group' was. This part of the office was strangely quiet. Not even the tapping of keyboard keys. Where was everybody?

The door banged open. An explosion of conversation filled the quiet office.

"Let's go, people. Hop to it. We have to have our asses on a plane out of here in less than ninety minutes. Got it?" A tall Hispanic man in a white shirt and striped tie strode into the office. He swept right past the aisle where Charlie sat with the chief and headed for an office door in the rear. "Where's the Commander? Chief!" He spun around. His dark eyes alight with an energetic fire.

His gaze settled on Charlie. "Who's this?"

Chief Ricard set down her file and stood. "Petty Officer Cutter. She's that linguist they brought on board." He directed his next words at her. "This is Special Agent Demarco."

Demarco scanned her for a moment, as if he were sizing her up. "You have your passport?"

"A passport? Where are we going?"

"This time we're headed to North Dakota. But tomorrow it might be Mongolia. You need to be prepared for any contingency."

"I applied for one back at DLI. Haven't gotten it yet."

"You're fresh from school?" Demarco's face curdled into

annoyance. "This is who they give us? Some wet-behind-the-ears newbie?"

Chief Ricard offered up her file. "You should see her test scores. They're off the charts."

"Just what I needed. Someone to babysit. We've got shit going down today, and this is the best they can do?"

Charlie's stomach churned. She wished she could be anywhere but in this office. Who in the hell sent her here if she clearly wasn't wanted?

"The commander put in the request. Maybe you should ask him," the chief said.

Demarco ran a hand through his short black hair. His handsome features marred by the obvious stress her presence was putting him under. He grunted. "Where is everyone? We need to get out of here, ASAP."

"Why do we need to go to North Dakota?" She'd just arrived here and now she was headed out somewhere else? She hadn't even had a chance to be briefed.

"You, sit." Demarco pointed at her. "Chief, you better as hell track down everyone now and make sure they're ready for transport." He headed toward Lisa. "Stormy, I need you to contact the doc and let her know we'll likely be bringing back samples. This is a big one."

Chief Ricard picked up the phone by his desk and started dialing. Lisa ran for a red phone on the wall marked 'secure.'

Bringing back samples of what? What was going on? Everyone had something to do except her. She was in the way. Lost. Clueless. She didn't like feeling out of the loop.

Chief hung up the phone, "The meeting's been over about ten minutes. Commander Orr and Lieutenant Kellerman should be here any second. Should I finish briefing Cutter?"

Demarco let out a breath. "Stormy can catch her up on

things once we're in the air. Right now I need your help making sure the equipment is ready before take-off."

Chief nodded, strode over to Lisa's desk, and dropped Charlie's file on it.

Lisa finished up on the phone. "Doc's ready for whatever we might bring back. She told me to remind you to take enough vials this time." She smirked. It was obvious to Charlie that Lisa found Demarco to be as much of a jerk as she did.

Demarco headed toward a door at the back of the office marked 'Supplies' and pulled out a set of keys. "Just finish getting ready, would you? Orr and Kellerman should be back any second, and we need to be prepped and packed."

Charlie bristled. What did this jackass know about her aptitude for the job? Someone clearly thought she was qualified, but she knew her place. She was new to the job and a third class Petty Officer with only an education to thank for her rank. For now, she had to suck it up. Later on she could prove her worth. If they needed a linguist, she sure as hell could show this special agent she had the chops to keep up with the team.

CHAPTER 4

LISA PICKED up the manila folder. "Want to take a seat?" She gestured at an empty office chair beside her. "I'll have to give you the short version."

Charlie made her way to the front of the office and took the offered chair.

Lisa opened the folder and peered at the same statistics and background Chief had perused moments earlier. She whistled. "Impressive."

"Right. I get it." Charlie's patience was wearing thin. Her first day, and she had no idea why she was here and was about to take a plane to North Dakota. Someone better start talking. "Are you going to brief me or do I need to find this Commander Orr?"

Lisa shot her a surprised look. "You're a go-getter." She set down the folder that contained Charlie's military records. "We don't have much time. I'll give you the quick down and dirty because we need to be on that plane. I'm thinking you aren't game for that until you know what we're up to. Am I close?"

Charlie relaxed and nodded. Finally, someone would shine a light on why she'd been diverted from her original orders.

"You've been assigned to NCIS-A or A Group, as we like to call it in here. Most of the people outside this office—the ones we shared the elevator with, the turnstiles, the parking lots—have no idea what we do."

Charlie took in the beige cubicles and fluorescent lighting. Looked a lot like any other boring office. "So what do you do?"

"We're a secret division that investigates extraterrestrial activity."

"Extraterrestrial activity?" What a crock. The rest of the office would jump out at any moment, yell surprise, and then spray her with Silly String. A first day joke on the newbie. She was no stranger to that. "You have to be joking."

Lisa spun her chair around to face her computer. She entered a password, and her computer desktop came alive. Splashed across the extra-wide screen was Lisa's email client. "This is where we're going today." She opened an email and clicked on a photo attachment. "A local farmer witnessed this crashing into a lake two nights ago in the middle of a pretty bad rain. Lots of flooding. It's going to be tricky to handle, but we've managed worse."

Charlie couldn't speak. On screen was a picture of a strange object, the size of a two-door compact car. Nothing about this object looked manufactured. It was green and gooey with a hatch-like opening. Strange markings covered part of it. A skinny man in a rain slicker stood to the side, knee-deep in muddy water. He was as white as a sheet.

"We're flying out there today to take samples, transport that thing to our lab, and give those guys a plausible story about what landed near this man's property." Lisa closed the file and shut down her computer.

"You're telling me this is something from outer space?"

"Stormy, let's go." A tall man in his late twenties with a military haircut, black-framed glasses, and dressed in civvies peeked around the cubicle. He gave Charlie a quick once over and then turned his focus back on Lisa. "Plane's ready."

Her new co-worker tucked Charlie's folder into a cardboard box on her desk. "We don't have a lot of time. Commander Orr needs to give you the full briefing." She grabbed the box.

Charlie stared at the odd object on the computer screen. Her mind was a blank. She didn't know what to think. Aliens? On earth? For real? If everyone around her weren't so serious, she'd probably burst out laughing.

Someone shut off the lights. "Let's go, people. We need to get the hell out of here."

Demarco. Jerk of the highest order.

She knew she wouldn't receive any answers from him. Lisa seemed kind enough and eager to give her the heads up on her new job. But Charlie agreed with Demarco—why in the heck did this office want a linguist? What possible input could she provide?

Charlie followed Lisa out the door. She had nothing on her, but her uniform, and now she was headed to North Dakota. For how long? She didn't even have a toothbrush with her for God's sake.

———

Seated inside the C-17 aircraft twenty minutes later, Charlie surveyed her new co-workers. They all bustled about the cabin, ignoring her as she sat on one of the jump seats along the wall.

Demarco stood near the front, clipboard in hand, checking off things as they were put away.

Did he ever stop scowling?

Lisa stuffed her cardboard box into a cargo net attached to

the wall, but grabbed Charlie's personnel file before finding her own seat near the front. Lisa immediately opened up the file and began to read.

Chief Ricard unloaded two large metallic cases and set them inside a cargo box the size of a garage freezer. His face appeared one shade darker and redder than when she'd first met him in the office. He plopped into a seat next to Lisa.

The youngish man with the glasses carried a military-style duffel bag and held an iPad in one hand. He took a seat across from Charlie, tucked his bag under his seat, and tapped away on the tablet.

A fifth person entered the aircraft. Like Chief Ricard, he wore a uniform—officer khakis with gold oak leaves on his collar. Charlie had not met him before, nor had he ridden with the rest of them over to the airstrip. This must be Commander Orr.

He carried a small bag, which he handed over to Demarco. Demarco checked something on his clipboard and then set the bag lightly into the cargo netting next to Lisa's cardboard box and some other soft-sided bags.

Orr headed her way. He had a slight smile on his face and extended his hand. "Welcome to the team, Petty Officer Cutter."

Charlie stood and accepted his hearty grip. "Thank you, sir." She didn't know what else to say. She had no idea why this man selected her as part of the strange office. She had so many questions no one seemed interested in answering.

He stood only about four inches taller than she, but his presence filled the cabin. "I'm sorry you had such an abrupt introduction to the shop. We haven't added a new teammate since Kellerman joined the team about nine months ago."

Kellerman must be the one with the glasses. The only name

she didn't recognize. "Is it always like this?" Everyone on the plane was filled with nervous energy. She could sense it. A much different atmosphere emanated from the group than when she'd met most of them an hour earlier.

Orr laughed. "You mean, dropping everything and flying off to the middle of nowhere?" He looked over his shoulder at Demarco who was still checking cargo and furrowing his brow as deeply as he could. "What say you, Demarco?"

The annoyingly handsome Demarco looked up from his clipboard, confusion clear in his eyes.

"Are we crazy sons of bitches?" the commander asked.

"Hell, yes." Demarco smiled, white teeth bright even in the yellowish fluorescent lighting that filled the cabin.

Charlie huffed inwardly—a gut, feminine reaction to that mega-watt smile.

He's a jerk, Charlie.

Orr took a seat next to Charlie and indicated she should sit back down. "I would rather have given you the full spiel in my office back in 1271, but right now we don't have that luxury. I know you're probably wondering why you were assigned to NCIS-A."

"I thought maybe you needed a really good Russian linguist." She thought proudly of her language proficiency scores and how she'd been looking forward to putting her language skills to use at something more practical than the academic career she'd been headed toward before she joined the Navy.

Orr smiled. "I haven't even looked at your scores, to tell you the truth."

Charlie's heart sank.

"I was more interested in your work before you joined the military. Your research into the Voynich Manuscript."

Charlie blinked. That wasn't what she'd been expecting to hear. Her pre-military life seemed as if it had happened decades ago. "You're interested in my linguistics work?" Her mind blipped back to her graduate school days. Living off of a small stipend, sitting through lectures on syntax, phonology and dialects, learning bits of Finnish, Chinese, and Swahili for fun. Seemed idyllic now.

"Kellerman, let me have your iPad."

The bookish Kellerman looked up from the tablet, and his face tinged pink. Charlie glanced at the surface of the tablet and caught a glimpse of a half-completed Sudoku matrix. She bit her lip to keep from laughing.

Kellerman cleared the screen with a finger tap and handed it across the cabin to Commander Orr.

Her new boss dug into a folder on the main screen of the iPad until he opened up a very familiar document—her master's thesis on the Voynich Manuscript.

The manuscript was a mysterious document that had mystified cryptographers for centuries. It consisted of more than two-hundred and forty pages of handwritten gobbledy-gook and illustrations and had been discovered in an Italian monastery by a Lithuanian bookseller named Voynich in 1912. Every expert, every master of code had failed to decipher the mysteries locked within the elaborate document. Many theorized it had been written by Leonardo da Vinci; others believed it was a bunch of junk. Charlie had been fascinated with the document since she'd first heard about the text in her freshman linguistics course at Baylor University.

"How did you find my thesis? I never finished it." The more she found out about this assignment, the more she wondered who had been pulling the strings. That thesis had been left on her laptop back at her parents' house. Once she'd quit grad school and abruptly joined the Navy, she thought it would be the end of that bit of writing.

"Your academic advisor told us he was disappointed you didn't finish."

"I was going nowhere with my analysis. The money was running out. I didn't feel like taking out a bigger student loan to end up with a half-baked idea."

"It's not half-baked. You have some great guesses in here that might lead to a—"

"A great guess is not what I'm interested in achieving, Commander Orr. When I first started that paper, I really thought I was onto something. Thought I saw a solution other people didn't see."

"But what if you did?" Orr flipped to the last page of her incomplete thesis.

Her failures in academia were not something she thought she'd be facing in her new assignment. "Why am I here, Commander Orr?"

He closed the file with a tap of his finger. "Your theories aren't bunk." He opened up a jpeg file. "The Voynich manuscript is a language. A real language. Not a code."

Orr handed her the iPad.

Charlie's gaze fixated on the picture he'd opened up. It was a blown up version of the photo Lisa had shown her earlier in the office. At this larger size, she could identify a familiar script scrawled across the unidentifiable greenish blob. The script was blurred, but the whorls and loops were definitely Voynich. "Where did this come from?" Only one document existed in the world with this writing. No other.

Orr took back the iPad. "We're about to show you."

CHAPTER 5

THE PILOT'S voice came across the loudspeaker. "We're cleared to go. Is everything secure?"

Orr headed to the front of the cabin to use the intercom and left Charlie in her seat with the iPad clutched in her sweaty hands. She couldn't take her eyes off the picture.

How could this possibly be? How could there be a strange green blob out in North Dakota that had the Voynich script on it?

She expanded the picture with her fingers to take a better look at the writings. Maybe Orr was mistaken. Maybe it only looked like Voynich script. When they arrived at the farm or wherever this blob was supposed to be, her boss would find out he'd recruited her for no reason. She was worthless to the team. All of this mystery about aliens and outer space...what would they do with her? Send her back to DLI? Give her new orders to SERE training in Maine? She'd wanted to be airborne and Survival, Evasion, Resistance and Escape training would be the first step in the right direction.

As she studied the blurry markings on the enlarged photo,

she sensed a presence next to her and got a whiff of his Axe cologne. She didn't realize men over twenty wore that stuff.

"Sorry the quality is crap." Kellerman took a seat next to her. "Someone needs to let Farmer Joe know that they have better cell phone cameras these days."

"Be straight with me. Have you guys really found evidence of aliens?" The blurry quality of the photo made it impossible for her to determine without a doubt if the writing was the same as Voynich or not. No point in going crazy looking at a pixelated green blob for the next several hours. May as well wait to see the real thing. Then she could make her determination as to whether or not Orr and the rest of NCIS-A made a mistake bringing her on board.

"We think so." He rubbed his hands down his pants legs. "I've seen some pretty crazy stuff since I got this assignment." He darted a glance toward the front of the cabin. "But I really should let Commander Orr read you in. He should have time after we take off."

The Top Secret security clearance she'd been given did not include access to all the details of every government project with a Top Secret designation. She still needed the additional Sensitive Compartmented Information access—or SCI—to actually understand the purpose and scope of her job.

"How long have you worked here?"

"Since about January."

"Are you Intelligence?"

Kellerman cracked a smile. "No, I started out in Cyber Warfare Engineering. I studied Computer Science at Northwestern. Not sure what you call me now. The paychecks keep coming, so it doesn't matter to me."

Charlie focused her gaze on Demarco who was now paging through her file. "Guess you already know everything about me." Demarco was probably looking for any weakness to peg her on: a sick day, a less-than-perfect score on her last advancement exam, an inspection failure. He seemed like the type who would relish that kind of discovery.

Kellerman's neck turned red. Bright red.

"Crew, listen up." Orr's voice echoed through the metal cylinder of the cabin.

Charlie wished she had more time to explore Kellerman's reaction to her comment.

The commander took a seat next to Demarco. "Time to strap in. We're cleared for takeoff. Just a reminder, this baby doesn't come with flight attendants and cocktail service. Snacks are in the cooler. Head's up front. We should be at Minot Air Force Base in about five hours. Then we have about a two-and-a-half hour drive to Camp Grafton. Any questions?"

Charlie raised her hand.

"Cutter."

"Are we staying overnight?"

"Yes, Petty Officer."

Demarco smirked.

Jackass.

She felt foolish for even asking. Of course they'd be staying there overnight. After more than seven hours of travel it'd be quite late in the evening even with the time change. She didn't want to bring up the fact she was the only one with no overnight bag in the cargo net. She swallowed the lump in her throat. "Thanks." She'd figure it out somehow. With Demarco around, she'd never admit to any failings.

"Anyone else?" Orr pulled the straps over his shoulders and connected them into the buckle across his lap. "We'll have our brief at 1330. Dismissed."

Kellerman crossed back to his original seat and dug around

in his pack for something. Guess any conversation was over with him. For a moment she wished she were back at DLI sitting in the chow hall with her flashcards learning more Russian vocabulary. For most of her adult life she'd been a researcher and a student. Her mind longed for the stimulation of new information. Five hours on a military plane with not even a seatmate to talk to sounded hellish. At least Kellerman had left her with the iPad.

She touched the close button on the photo of the blurry blob. If the plane was taking them where this blob was, she'd learn more if she saw the thing in person. Sure, the writing looked like Voynich, but it could be random markings for all she knew. Until Orr or someone else on this plane gave her the background about the object, she was only along for the ride. She needed to know origins, how this was related to aliens, and what their expectation was of her in this new role as resident linguistics 'expert.'

Her advisor at Baylor would've been a better choice for this assignment. Professor Klingman had introduced her to the strange manuscript and encouraged her to continue exploring its mysteries in her graduate research. Whenever she'd been discouraged, he'd helped her through it. Maybe she could suggest the professor as a replacement candidate if this didn't work out.

The memory of the day she'd told Klingman she wasn't going to finish her master's degree made her cringe. She'd never been one to fail at anything. When she showed up at home in San Antonio with her laptop and all her belongings, her father had reminded her of that. *Cutters don't quit, Charlie.*

She tucked away the memory of that day in the back of her mind. It brought up too many negative feelings.

Charlie focused her attention on the iPad, found the

Sudoku app Kellerman had been using, and started up a game. Everything else seemed to be password protected. Without knowing its possibly confidential contents, she wasn't sure if she should be handling the device. Could the photo of the blob really be unclassified?

———

Charlie awoke to a hand on her shoulder.

"Hey, the Commander wants to brief you now."

Charlie opened her eyes and saw Lisa bent over her. When did she fall asleep? She sat up quickly, embarrassed she'd drifted off with a bunch of strangers around her. The iPad had disappeared from her lap. She touched her hair.

"You look fine. Come on." Lisa urged her toward the back of the plane where Commander Orr and Special Agent Demarco waited.

Great.

Her mouth was dry. She wished she had a minute to look at herself in a mirror. Curiosity, however, drove her forward. She used the line of jump seats along the wall of the aircraft to guide her. Unlike commercial aircraft, this plane had no windows. Beneath her feet, recessed handles lined the floor indicating more storage compartments. To make sure she didn't stumble, she kept her eyes on the floor.

"Have a seat, Cutter." Orr gestured to a more traditional-looking airline seat in a row of six.

She picked one, leaving some distance.

Demarco handed her a piece of paper on a clipboard. "I need you to read this and sign it."

She read through the document. Along with all the warnings about prosecution if she revealed any classified material, it gave her access to SCI documents marked with both the KLONDIKE and YARDARM control systems. She signed her name at the bottom and dated it.

Demarco took it from her, signed his name next to hers, slid it into a leather briefcase, and snapped it shut. "What you are about to read cannot be talked about outside of this plane or the office. Do you understand?"

"I've been through the clearance process. I signed the read in document. Yes, I understand." So far only Demarco rubbed her the wrong way. She bit her lip to avoid saying anymore. It wouldn't be good to give him a reason to dislike her more than he already did.

"This will explain things to you." Orr handed her a red manila folder full of papers. "If you have any questions, let me know."

She took the folder from him. "I will. Thanks."

Orr smiled; Demarco scowled. They both left her sitting in the back of the plane and made their way forward to their seats.

She sat for a moment looking at the red folder in her lap. So NCIS-A tracked aliens. Even if she didn't one-hundred percent believe it was true, the contents of the folder should tell her what she needed to know. Then she could judge for herself if she'd ended up in some wacky secret branch of the Navy or if this was real.

Charlie opened the red folder. Her hands sweated. Her brain told her aliens did not exist. She wanted to read the contents with an open mind, but it was hard to do when the word 'alien' only invoked a mental picture of Spielberg's E.T.

The first things inside the folder were a series of pictures. Different photos than the one on the iPad. The light quality was terrible, but the object in the foreground was unmistakable

—another pod. She flipped the photo over to see if it was marked on the back.

When was this taken?

Nothing. No markings.

She scrutinized the picture again. One close-up photo of the pod had the glare of a flash splattered across its dark green surface. The Voynich-like markings were clearly visible. Her finger traced across the familiar letter pattern.

There had been another pod before this one.

She set the picture aside. Eager to read the documents that filled the folder. The first was a report. The date in the upper right hand corner stated it was written in July 2022—one year earlier.

TOP SECRET KLONDIKE

To: Director, Naval Criminal Investigative Service, Mr. S. Trainor

From: LCDR Jacob McDowell

Subject: Unidentified Object—NAVSECGRU Fort Madison, Iowa

Site report from NAVSECGRU Fort Madison indicates crash landing of Unidentified Object (UO) at 2230 hours on 15 JUL 2022. Witnesses attested to loud noises, fire before UO landed in the Mississippi River.

Petty Officer Ledbetter and Seaman Conlon were first on scene. Ledbetter and Conlon both described a large round object about eight feet in diameter. Organic in nature, green or black in color. Hull had been breached by the crash. UO disintegrated in

*rain and flood waters before team arrival. Unable to attain spec-
imen due to degradation in the field.*

*Photographs attached to report show size, shape, color and
possible writing-like markings on external shell.*

*Ledbetter testified to seeing fleeing figure, which emerged
from UO after crash. No clear description given beyond esti-
mated height (6 feet) and anthropomorphic shape. Search of the
surrounding areas revealed no tracks or trace of anything
coming from the crash site.*

Conlon did not corroborate Ledbetter's testimony.

*Further investigation unwarranted due to lack of evidence.
Filed under UO until further identification is possible.*

Suggested actions: None at this time.

The report was thin. Charlie had been hoping for more details.
Many questions had popped into her mind. The photos were
the only evidence of this first pod. She wished she could inter-
rogate the two sailors who claimed to have seen the crash.

The rest of the folder was filled with a dozen local accounts
of the same mysterious crash in 2022. People who lived near
the site were interviewed, their details written down by hand
on sheets of lined paper. Names, addresses, and phone
numbers of people who probably had forgotten all about the
strange fiery crash during the storm.

Charlie wanted more. This file told her nothing. Why all
the secrecy and special handling when this read like another
Roswell incident? It was a junk report written by an over-
worked Naval officer who most likely wanted to escape the rain
and go home to his wife and kids.

Where was the explanation for the current situation?
Where were the details of the 'pod' and its origins? Certainly an

expert in extraterrestrial life would've weighed in on this craziness by now?

This was her briefing into NCIS-A?

Charlie flipped through a dozen of the handwritten reports. The very last page caught her attention. Another classified document from a year ago.

TOP SECRET KLONDIKE

To: Director, National Security Agency
From: LCDR D. Orr
Subject: New Investigative Division

Requesting creation of new investigative division under the purview of NCIS in order to respond to recent events. Request made for the following reasons:

Second UO sighting identical to report from 15 JUL 2022

Additional evidence obtained that points to OTE (Other-than-Earth) origins

Samples obtained that need further study outside regular channels

Implications could be substantial; therefore, additional classification and study is necessary.

New division would require two additional cleared personnel for support. Reference Report #3A15972C for further details of related events.

Charlie leaned back in her seat. Stamped at the top and bottom of the document all in caps was the word YARDARM—the SCI designator for classified material associated with NCIS-A.

The NCIS-A division was brand new. No wonder the file was thin. Or maybe this was only the part of the documentation that pertained to her job on this team.

Where was the additional information about this secondary event? This meant the pod in North Dakota was pod number three. There were no more documents in the file. Did they have pictures from the second pod? Was this pod also covered in Voynich-like markings? Did they retrieve any other evidence? Did anyone else see a possible human-like figure emerge?

Adrenaline coursed through her at the possibilities.

Charlie picked up the blurry photographs again. She needed to start taking notes on this stuff. If she was brought on the team to figure out the meaning of the strange symbols on the pods, then she would need to work on crafting a database. One of the reasons deciphering the Voynich text had been so daunting was the lack of multiple documents using the same symbol system. The more examples of writing she had, the possibility of cracking the code grew more likely.

Despite her doubts about the existence of aliens, she needed to take her job seriously. This is why she'd left her graduate studies, didn't she? To find something meaningful in life, more exciting. Plus, she'd never been able to truly uncover all the mysteries the Voynich document held. Here was her opportunity. The keys to solving the mystery. Right at her fingertips. No deadlines. No professor breathing down her neck about proving her thesis. No one telling her she was wrong.

As part of this team, she was the linguistics expert. That is what Commander Orr told her. No one would question her theories. She'd have full authority to follow any rabbit trail she liked.

Maybe this whole extraterrestrial thing was crazy. Maybe it was nothing more than a handful of kooks running around meeting with nutjobs and conspiracy theorists. She was only a cog in a much larger wheel, which meant she could focus on her one little piece of it and leave the big stuff to someone else.

There was comfort in that.

She closed the file, pictures and all, and headed back to her seat for a pen and a notebook.

"Whoa, hold on there, Cutter." Demarco snatched the folder from her hands.

"Hey, I need that." His eye line was slightly higher than hers. Did it bother him they were almost the same height? "I need to take some notes."

Commander Orr was deep in conversation with Chief Ricard at the front of the plane. Charlie wished she could shove Demarco out of the way and sit down with the commander for a franker discussion about her job and these old reports.

"This is classified material." Demarco's eyes snapped. "You've read it; now it needs to be checked back in before we land."

The patronizing son of a bitch. "Commander Orr brought me on because you don't have anyone on the team with my kind of skills. Why don't you let me do my job?"

"I'm the head of security on this team, Petty Officer." Demarco emphasized her rank with a curl of his lip. "It's *my* job to make sure our documents are secured properly."

Petty Officer Storm appeared out of nowhere and put a hand on Demarco's forearm. "Give her a few minutes to take notes, Angel. You'll have time to lock it up."

Lisa's quiet words calmed the Special Agent. "Fine." Demarco's voice came down a notch or two. "You've got exactly ten minutes."

Charlie took back the folder. "Thank you." Her shoulders had tensed up. She forced herself to relax. Thank God for Lisa.

Clearly, she knew how to calm the savage beast. So much for not having to prove herself anymore. Demarco might be harder to win over than the Linguistics Department at Baylor.

Demarco turned and headed back to his seat.

"His bark is worse than his bite," Lisa whispered. "You just have to know how to handle him."

"Thanks for the help. Guess I've got a long way to go before I fit into the team." Charlie sat in her seat, and Lisa joined her. "I feel as if I've got a lot of catching up to do."

Lisa smiled, which exposed a gap between her front teeth. "You'll pick it up. Look, if it makes you feel any better, Demarco told me I was a glorified secretary on my first day and that my most important job was picking up his coffee order."

"You're kidding."

"I wish I were. Demarco's one of those guys who wants everything to go back the way it used to be: men in charge; women in the back seat."

"Guess I shouldn't be hoping for much, then."

"Exactly. That's who the guy is. You can't change him. He might look young, but he's got the mind of my grandfather when it comes to the role of women in the work place. Don't let it get to you."

"I'll try not to."

Lisa squeezed her hand. "You'll be just fine." She caught sight of Commander Orr waving her toward him and took her leave.

Focusing back on her notes, Charlie wrote TOP SECRET YARDARM at the top and bottom of a page of blank paper she'd managed to find. Scrutinizing the faded photographs, she began creating a sketch of each symbol she could discern. At some point, she'd need to craft a more permanent document, but for now this would do.

"Would this help?" Quiet Kellerman leaned across the aisle and handed her a spiral notebook. "Demarco passed these out to us. I never use mine."

"Thanks." Charlie accepted the plain black notebook.

"Don't forget to give it to him when you're done. He can store it in the locker before we land."

"I have to go through him every time I want to access my notes?" Charlie imagined the glowering face of Demarco. That wasn't something she looked forward to.

"When we're traveling. When we're working in the office, you can leave your notes in your desk."

"Right. Secured office."

"Right." Kellerman cracked the tiniest of smiles.

Determined to prove herself a worthy asset to the team, Charlie sketched out her notes as quickly as possible. Then, she confidently headed straight to Demarco, handed him the folder and her notebook, and looked him straight in the eye. "Done. You can store these now."

Special Agent Demarco quietly took the materials and gave a curt nod.

Charlie sighed inwardly. One chink from his armor had been removed. Only a thousand more chinks to go.

CHAPTER 6

THE C-17 LANDED LIKE AN ELEPHANT, heavily and with no elegance. The savage jolt woke Charlie from a fitful sleep. Her stomach lurched. Nausea grew. The spare lunch Lisa had handed out to everyone—peanut butter sandwiches and a bottle of water—didn't quite fill the empty, nervous pit inside her.

A wisp of hair slid into her eyes. Charlie adjusted a bobby pin and re-secured the loose strand into her French braid. Her white navy skirt held a days' worth of wrinkles in it. With nothing to change into, she considered the possibilities. Would they be checking into a motel where she could hang her uniform in the bathroom and mist out the wrinkles with hot water from the shower? Or were they going to rush straight to the scene to investigate the mysterious pod? Although she was eager to examine this 'alien' pod for herself, she worried about the lack of proper gear.

"Minot reports a temperature of eighty-five degrees. Steady rain." The pilot's scratchy voice came across the intercom. "Please stay belted in until we give you the go-ahead."

"Heads up, folks. We have half a day before nightfall and a

lot of ground to cover." Commander Orr appeared invigorated and alert—his regulation haircut perfectly combed and looking crisp, uniform clean and free of wrinkles. "Stormy, you show Cutter the ropes when we arrive on scene."

What a relief to hear she'd be teamed up with Lisa. They'd gotten on well together in the short span of time they'd known each other. Maybe because Charlie was the only other woman on the team, but for now that was enough to carry her through the day.

The plane came to an abrupt halt.

After a few moments of silence, the pilot's voice crackled on the intercom again. "All clear. All clear."

Everyone unbelted. Charlie followed suit.

Lieutenant Kellerman packed up his gear. Demarco, up in front of the plane with the commander, fiddled with the crate of secured items. Chief Ricard removed boxes and bags from the netting and handed a few things off to Lisa.

Charlie had nothing to collect and no clue what her job should be at this stage. She ran her tongue across her teeth and wished for a piece of mint gum. "Do you need any help?" Kellerman was closest to her.

He hoisted his bag over his shoulder. "That's okay. I got it." He headed for the back of the plane behind the rest of her co-workers.

Charlie followed Kellerman with her meager belongings in hand. Rain pounded on the roof of the big plane, and the drops sounded like gunshots. She wished she'd brought a jacket with her that morning to the office. The weather had been warm and dry in D.C., and the extra layer had seemed unnecessary. Her shoulders slumped.

The back of the C-17 opened up like a trap door. Rain poured down in sheets. A gust of wind blew into the cabin.

They'd landed on the tarmac about a half mile from any building or shelter. Charlie set her cover on her head, glad for the bit of protection it gave her. As she took the ramp one step at a time, she anticipated the drenching she was about to receive with dread.

Everyone else wore rain gear and didn't seem to mind the weather.

Charlie stepped into the storm, and the rain pummeled her black cardigan sweater which covered her white cotton shirt. At least the humidity from the storm might release some of the wrinkles in her uniform. The wind whipped at the edge of her skirt. She put her head down and caught sight of a bus waiting about fifty yards from the plane.

Dry warmth embraced her. Charlie, startled, looked to her right. Special Agent Demarco wrapped his trench coat around her shoulders. "Where's your coat?"

"I don't have one."

"You need to learn to be prepared, Cutter." He slowed his stride to match hers as they approached the waiting bus. "Our team has to be ready to move when the call comes in. There's no time to screw around packing a bag. Next time, you come to the office with your gear."

Charlie pulled the edges of the coat closer around her body. "I will." Even though Demarco had rubbed her the wrong way from the start, the gesture had been a kind one. Maybe he wasn't so bad after all.

Demarco waited until she stepped up into the bus first and then followed. "I'm sure Stormy can loan you a few things once we're done for the day. Keep the coat until we're back in D.C. I've got a poncho in my bag I can use."

"Thanks." Charlie took the first empty seat at the front of

the bus. She scooted to the window, assuming Demarco would join her.

He slipped past her, however, and sat down across from the commander further back. The two of them immediately were deep in conversation.

She slid her arms into the coat Demarco had given her. He'd noticed her dilemma and had offered a helping hand. That went a long way to bridging the gap between them. In such a small office, it wouldn't be good to start off on the wrong foot. Maybe she'd misjudged the man.

Charlie stared out the window at the storm. A mystery waited for them a few hours away. Until she saw the pod with her own eyes, she wouldn't believe there was anything alien about it. It didn't matter what the classified materials revealed to her. She'd spent months with the Voynich manuscript. Everything about it said 'earth' to her.

She took her phone out of her purse and searched online for the manuscript. It had been a couple of years since she'd laid eyes on it. The document used to be as familiar to her as her own brother.

She found the page she was looking for: an intricate image of a dragon with a long, curling tail, standing on a globe with three flaming orbs inside it. The dragon had a wound that rained droplets of blood on the orbs, which looked as if they sat in a lake of blue water. Four columns of writing appeared underneath the colorful artwork.

"What's that?" Lisa leaned over the back of the seat.

Charlie held the phone out for Lisa to see the screen better. "It's a page from an old manuscript."

"Can you read that stuff?" Lisa pointed at the writing on the ancient page.

"No, but I was working on it a few years ago." Charlie

tapped on the screen to black it out. Her intention had not been to dredge up old regrets; she'd only wanted to familiarize herself with the writings to be prepared for whatever they encountered at Camp Grafton.

"I'm sorry." Lisa scrambled around the seat and sat next to her. "I didn't mean to pry."

"That's okay." Charlie knew Lisa's questions were well meaning. The last thing she needed to do was push away a possible friend. "Commander Orr thinks I can help decipher some of this stuff for you. I want to make sure I'm prepared. It's been awhile since I've worked with these documents."

"You've been at the language school, right?"

"Yeah. In Monterey."

"Not a bad gig."

Charlie nodded. "It's a beautiful place—expensive, but beautiful." She thought of the views of Monterey Bay from the 'hill' on which the military language school was built. On sunny days it was like paradise. She could walk to the beach or the pier, stroll the small downtown of Monterey or walk a little further into Pacific Grove. Giving up six hours of her day for language class and a few hours a night to study was a good deal compared to other Navy training schools. "What about you? Where did you go for training?"

"Florida." She smiled and flashed her gapped teeth.

"That's not so bad either."

Lisa shrugged. "Pensacola's okay. We were about fifteen minutes from the beach, though."

"Nice." Charlie imagined the warmth and humidity of sunny Florida. Monterey might've been beautiful, but it also could be cold and foggy for most of the summer.

"Nice if you have a car. I was pretty much stuck on base for two months."

Charlie reconsidered the idea. "That would suck."

"Exactly."

Conversation lulled. They both stared out the window at the passing landscape. As they moved further away from the base in Minot, the storm slowed to a drizzle.

"I was hoping it would clear up before we got to Grafton," Lisa said. "Last time, we had to do all of our work in the rain. By the time we were done collecting all of our samples, taking pictures, and interviewing witnesses, I was soaked to the bone."

"Will Commander Orr give me an assignment when we arrive? I'm not sure what I'm supposed to do."

"Demarco's pretty much the point man. He's been with the group longer than I have." Lisa was fully engaged now. "The commander is kind of our management guy. He interacts with the higher ups, keeps them off our backs."

"What about the Chief?"

"He's in charge of all our equipment. If we need anything, a camera, an iPad, whatever, we check it out from him. He logs it in the book. He's also the one who does the on-site repairs. Like our personal MacGuyver."

Charlie smiled inwardly at the comparison. Richard Dean Anderson's attractive head superimposed onto Chief Ricard's portly body. "And Kellerman's the computer nerd."

"I heard he came from an assignment at Area 51 before he ended up in our office."

"He didn't mention that detail." Charlie tucked that away for future reflection.

"In case you didn't notice already, he's a bit introverted. He's not the biggest conversationalist. I leave him alone and let him do his thing. That seems to be what he prefers."

Demarco appeared in the aisle next to Lisa. He turned and faced the back of the bus and interrupted their conversation with an announcement. "Everyone, we'll be at Grafton in about five minutes. Our goal is to collect as many samples as we can. We're hoping for better luck than last time. With the rain slowing down, there's a good chance we'll be able to bring something back this time. Keep your eyes peeled. Anything out of the ordinary, report it to me immediately. Commander Orr will be in charge of interviewing witnesses. Stormy, you help him out. Kellerman, I want you and Chief in charge of photos and retrieving any samples at the scene. Be careful not to contaminate anything." He pointed a finger at Charlie. "Cutter, you're with me."

Although Charlie was grateful to Demarco for loaning her his coat, she wasn't so sure about having to work with him. He'd shown nothing but scorn for her and her background since she'd walked in the door.

"Let's not disappoint Dr. Stern this time." Demarco finished his speech and headed to the back of the bus.

"Dr. Stern, is she the doctor mentioned back in the office?" Charlie asked Lisa.

Lisa filled in the knowledge gap. "She's our forensics expert. She likes to stay in D.C. as she's pretty attached to her work."

The bus took an exit off the highway marked 'Devils Lake.' After a few miles they drove across a spit of land that had water surrounding them on either side. The land was flat for miles around. Not a hill or mountain in sight. The choppy, dark lake reflected the stormy sky above. The rain had slowed to a mist, and a bit of blue sky attempted to break through in the distance.

Nerves took over. After today, she might believe there were extraterrestrials on earth. The possibility was frightening, but exciting at the same time.

The bus turned through the gates at the entrance to Camp

Grafton, a National Guard station. They drove past the guard shack and parked near a low lying brown building. An officer in BDUs waited for them in the rain.

"Are you ready?" Lisa whispered.

The bus door opened.

"Yes," Charlie heard herself say as she stood up and headed out into the wet and damp to face whatever waited there for her. "I'm ready."

CHAPTER 7

CHARLIE SHIVERED and followed Demarco through the woods that lined the edge of Camp Grafton. One section of the National Guard installation sat along the edge of Devils Lake where the pod had been found by a local farmer whose land abutted the camp. A vigilant National Guardsman, who'd been stationed there the night before in case of flooding from the storm, arrived on scene not much later to capture additional photos of the find.

"Pick up the pace, Cutter." Demarco pushed through the heavy brush and trees that blocked their route. He shifted a heavy backpack as he moved. "We don't have much time."

"I'm trying," Charlie puffed.

They had left Orr and Lisa back at the bus. When they arrived, the officer in charge of Camp Grafton had been waiting for them and led the commander and Charlie's new friend into a brown brick building where witnesses waited to be interviewed.

Charlie kept up as best she could with Demarco's blistering pace. She thought she was in good shape, but he somehow managed to stay several yards ahead of her no matter how hard she pushed herself. The heavy bag she'd been encumbered with back at the bus wasn't helping things any.

Although Chief and Kellerman were supposed to be taking photos at the scene of the crash, Ricard didn't even try to keep up with Demarco and Kellerman had hung back with his team mate. So Charlie and Demarco had pressed ahead without them.

"What are we looking for?" She wanted to have some idea of his expectations for her.

Demarco didn't answer.

The rain had slowed to a fuzz. Wet drops slipped from Charlie's cover and rolled down her collar. They had to be almost there. The sound of gentle waves lapping against the shore made that clear. She shifted the heavy bag to her opposite hand.

Demarco disappeared into the trees.

Charlie followed his footsteps, which had made obvious impressions in the sandy dirt.

"Hey! Cutter, hurry up." Demarco's booming bass voice split the quiet of the woods. "We have something here."

Charlie's heart sputtered unevenly. Her mind flashed to the Voynich Manuscript. Was this going to be the moment she made a discovery? Her dream in graduate school had been to crack the code, translate the text, and wow the world with her linguistic capabilities. She'd be able to write herself a ticket to any university she wanted. The scholars who'd studied the text for decades would be bowled over by the young graduate student and her work.

The trees thinned. Charlie burst through the tangle of branches and bushes to find herself on a rocky strip of land with grasses drowning in flood waters. The lake in front of her was muddy with choppy waves. Demarco stood about fifty yards away. She headed in his direction.

As she edged closer, her gut tightened. A gigantic, lopsided pile of green goop in the shape of a sliced open watermelon sat in about two feet of water.

The pod.

"Damn." Charlie couldn't help herself. Looking at the pictures and reading the reports hadn't really resonated with her. But seeing a pod in person—that rendered her mute. Goose bumps rose on her arms and scalp. Aliens were real.

"Stop gawking and start taking notes." Demarco crouched down in the knee deep water to take a closer look. "Dr. Stern is going to flip out." He touched the edge of the pod with his fingers and rubbed them together. "Slimy. Organic for sure."

Charlie dug into her bag and yanked out one of the notebooks that had been kept in the security box on the plane. She carefully wrote "TOP SECRET YARDARM" at the top and bottom of the first page. Her hand trembled. She took a deep breath. Freaking out would not help at this point. She'd only piss off Demarco and screw up her first day on the job. She needed to be as calm as the Special Agent seemed to be.

"Pod is approximately eight feet across and made up of dark green organic material. The roof is missing. No signs of life." Demarco circled around it, stepping deeper into the lake. He ran his hand along the pod as he walked and filled a test tube with the goo.

"Do you see any markings?" Charlie moved closer to the object, peering inside. To her unschooled gaze, the green lump of gunk inside looked like a seat of some kind. Rising from the floor were structures that could be mechanical pieces. Levers and knobs set in green goo. "Whoa, did you look inside?"

"Stay back." Demarco noticed how close she was to it. "We

don't know if this could be harmful stuff or what. Where the hell is the Chief? This thing is disintegrating fast."

As if the pod heard him, a chunk of it slid into the lake and disappeared.

"Fuck." Demarco was now up to his hips in the murky lake. "Do you have a phone on you?" He wiped his hands on his poncho and placed the test tube in his pants pocket.

"Yes." Charlie pulled her smart phone from the pocket of his trench coat. Strange that Demarco didn't want her to approach it, but yet he had pod slime all over his hands. "Want me to take pictures?"

"Yes. Be warned, though, you'll have to hand your phone over to the Chief. Once those pictures are taken, you've got classified material on it. You won't get it back."

She hesitated.

"We'll give you a new one. Don't worry."

She snapped pictures of the exterior from the shore and the strange interior. She used the zoom feature to take up close photos of the seat-like structure inside. When she used the same zoom on the mechanical-looking parts, her breath caught in her throat. "The markings. Do you see them?" She stared at the screen of her smart phone and snapped several photos. "It's the same."

They were Voynich-like markings for sure. She'd recognize the loops and whorls anywhere. How could it be that a book written hundreds of years ago could have the same writing as this pod? Could the manuscript really have been written by an alien, stranded centuries ago on earth? And if there was writing on the inside of the pod, then couldn't it be possible it contained life from outer space? Thinking, breathing, intelligent life?

The whole idea of the discovery and its implications for the world overwhelmed her. So unbelievable. So remarkable.

My God.

One whole side of the pod caved in, falling on top of the interior structures and burying the writing she'd only just photographed.

"Dammit." She took as many pictures as she could and stepped deeper into the lake, her shoes filling with water. The pod disintegrated rapidly. Once the side collapsed, the lake poured in and weakened the object further.

"Charlie, where's Demarco?" Kellerman called from the shore. He and the Chief had finally arrived.

"What?" When had Demarco taken off? They'd both been examining the pod. Far down the beach she could see a figure about to disappear behind a curve of land that followed the edge of the lake. "Demarco!" She didn't know why she bothered calling his name. He was already too far away to hear her. "Here, take my phone and snap more photos before this thing is gone."

Charlie waded back to shore and tossed her phone to Kellerman. What had Demarco observed that caused him to leave the scene?

Kellerman caught the phone before it hit the gravel. "Sorry it took us so long. Chief left his tripod in the bus, and we had to go back."

"Whatever." Charlie's gaze focused on Demarco. He'd almost disappeared from view. "I took some good ones before it started to fall apart. You finish up. I'll be back in a minute. Take more samples."

Kellerman said something to her, but she wasn't listening.

She trotted in her soggy dress shoes toward the shrinking figure of Demarco. Not wanting to be slowed down, she'd left her heavy bag on the shore with Kellerman and Chief. "Demarco, wait!"

The figure didn't stop.

What the hell? Why didn't he say anything to her? What had he seen?

She focused on the point of land a half-mile in front of her. He'd managed to travel quite far in a short period of time. She pushed herself to run harder. Her breath came out in ragged gasps, and her lungs burned. Swimming was more her style, but she'd had to run in Boot Camp, and that wasn't too long ago.

She leapt over drift wood and rocks that were scattered along the beach. In some places, the rising waters of the lake practically buried any possible path along the shore. She'd had to slow down a few times to skirt the flooding by entering into the wood line and find a new place to continue.

The figure she'd been watching at the edge of the lake disappeared around the bend, but now she was only about a fifty yards from the spot. It had definitely been Demarco she'd seen. As she'd closed in on him, she recognized his poncho flapping in the breeze.

She reached the bend and made a turn, hoping she'd see him not too far ahead.

He'd vanished.

Uncertain where to go next, she made an abrupt stop. Her feet throbbed in her shoes. Not exactly made for running with their flat soles and zero arch support. She'd probably regret the run in the morning.

Where did you go, Demarco?

She scanned the rocky strip of beach. Only about a foot of land remained uncovered by the rising lake.

Footsteps in the sand.

Yes!

She'd found his trail.

As she approached the tracks, she stopped dead. Her heart fluttered.

Next to Demarco's boot prints was a distinct second set of prints. Not another set of shoe prints, but prints of someone who'd passed through here barefoot.

Her mind couldn't comprehend what she was seeing. The feet that had made the second set of prints didn't look human. Didn't look like anything she'd ever seen. There were two 'toes' with a split down the middle that reminded her of a pig's hoof. Yet the print had a distinct heel and arch.

What in the hell was Demarco following?

Charlie set aside the fear that set in when she saw those strange prints in the sand. She had to find Demarco. Had he seen the creature that made them?

She followed them to the edge of the brush and woods that lined the lake. Demarco had headed this way. Would she find him nearby?

Instinct told her to remain quiet. She drew on her limited experience with hunting. Her father had wanted her to become as expert a marksman as her brother, but she couldn't stand the idea of killing something. He'd taken her on three deer hunting trips, and all three she'd ended up in tears. Her brother would kneel on the ground next to his kill, and she'd be hiding in the tent waiting for it all to be over.

The crack of a breaking branch startled her. The noise had come from the woods. Was it Demarco? Or the creature?

Fear kept her immobilized. She didn't know if she could move forward. Everything inside her was telling her to stay put and wait for help to arrive. This was her first day, dammit. Her first day. She didn't know protocols. No one had warned her of this possibility. She had no weapon, no training, and now she was in an incredibly vulnerable position.

She took a step back.

Another crack.

Her breathing sounded loud to her own ears. She made each breath as shallow as she could. Her gaze focused on the trees and shrubs in front of her.

"Cutter. What are you doing here?" Demarco stepped from the woods.

Relief flooded her. "You left me on the beach. I saw you way down here and thought you could use some help." Charlie felt the fool. She had no way to provide any help had he needed it. Had he found the creature that made the prints? His calm demeanor told her 'no.'

"Why did you abandon your assignment? Did you take enough pictures? Has the pod disintegrated?" The special agent wiped his sweaty forehead with the back of his hand. His hard gaze unnerved her.

"Kellerman and Chief showed up. I left the camera with them." She squinted at her superior. The sun had broken through the heavy cloud cover and shone in her eyes. She couldn't hold in her question any longer. "Did you find it?"

"Find what?" He stood still with his face in shadow. Charlie had a hard time reading his expression.

His answer knocked her back. Her confidence in what she'd seen, shaken. "Whatever made those weird footprints on the beach. It looked as if you were following them." She shifted her weight onto her other foot. "Is that why you came down here?"

"I thought I saw something...a movement. A shape. I wasn't sure. So I thought I'd better check it out." He brushed past her.

"Then when I saw these, I thought I was on to something." He crouched down in the tall grass that rimmed the beach and parted it to reveal another of the strange prints.

Charlie hunkered down next to him. "Yes, I saw them, too. The alien. He left them here." Her thoughts skipped ahead. "The pod landed last night during the storm. The creature escaped from the pod and ran from the scene. But how did his footprints survive the rain and the flooding? Shouldn't they be washed away by now?"

"Whoa, slow down, Cutter. You're getting ahead of yourself. These are just shoe prints."

"Shoe prints?" Charlie couldn't believe it. She'd been fooled by a pair of shoes?

"When I saw these prints, I was in the same place you were. I headed into the woods, and then realized I'd let my imagination run away with me."

Demarco did not seem like the type to have any imagination whatsoever. Pressed pants, shined shoes, fresh haircut.

"Once I entered the woods, the sand turned into mud. Deeper prints. More definition. Definitely shoe prints. Some kind of brand that looks Japanese with the split toe." He cocked a half-smile at her. "I appreciate your enthusiasm. We need someone like that on our team. Commander Orr is always wrapped up in the red tape whenever we arrive on scene and Chief can't keep up with the pace. This time, though, it was a wild goose chase. It happens."

Charlie touched the print. "Guess I have to learn to slow down. Be more observant." She wiped the sand from her hands and stood. "All this alien stuff is new to me. I only want to do a good job." She could've kicked herself for revealing her worries to a man who'd already doubted her usefulness to the team.

"Why don't you head back to the crash site. Kellerman and

the Chief are going to need your help." He pulled a small electronic device from his jacket pocket. "I need to take temperature measurements—air, water. You go on ahead of me, and I'll catch up."

She needed to grow accustomed to the ups and downs that came with this job. How silly of her to think they'd figure out the meaning of these pods on her very first day. "Will do. Sorry for dropping the ball." Did Kellerman manage to take more pictures before the pod deteriorated completely?

"It's all right, Cutter. This job has a steep learning curve. You're only beginning to scratch the surface." Demarco walked down to the water's edge and stuck the tip of his device into the lake. "We have to make sure we collect plenty of samples to bring back with us. This is the most intact pod we've ever encountered."

Cutter took that as her cue to leave Demarco to his tests. "I'll let Chief know where you are. See you back at the bus later?"

"Yes. I shouldn't be too much longer."

Demarco took sample after sample of lake water. How many samples could he possibly need? Charlie turned and headed back toward the crash site. She could see tall, skinny Kellerman and short, pudgy Chief Ricard circling the pod remains. Time for her to pull her weight.

CHAPTER 8

"HEY, where did you run off to?" Kellerman caught sight of Charlie as she returned to the beach where the mission had begun. He held an open case full of test tubes stuffed with green goo from the pod.

"I thought Demarco needed help." She tilted her head toward the distant point of the lakeshore where she'd seen the special agent thirty minutes earlier. "Turns out, he was fine without me. Did you take any more photos?" She hoped Kellerman would drop the subject of Demarco and focus on their assignment. Disappointment lingered after finding out the prints were nothing more than a shoe tread.

"A few. I have your phone around here somewhere." Kellerman held the heavy case against his side with one hand while he searched his pockets.

She expected him to drop the case any moment.

"It's okay." She reached for it, intending to rescue it, if he lost grip. "Demarco told me I wouldn't get it back anyway."

Confusion clouded Kellerman's expression. The case slipped. She flinched.

"Classified material."

"Sure." He shifted the case back into a more solid two-handed grip. "Guess you're going to need a new phone."

As if on cue, her phone played the distinctive Russian National Anthem she'd chosen as her ring tone when she'd gotten into the DLI Russian program. It was definitely in one of Kellerman's pockets. "Sorry." Her face heated. "You can let it go to voicemail."

Kellerman jumped at the simultaneous vibration. "Back pocket. Grab it." He turned slightly to make it easier for her.

"That's okay. I don't mind if it goes to voicemail." She wasn't about to dig into her male co-worker's back pocket to reclaim her phone.

"I got it." Chief came up from behind and snatched the phone from Kellerman's pants. "Heads up." He tossed it in Charlie's direction.

She fumbled it, and it fell into the sand. "Whoops." When she bent over to retrieve it, she saw her father's name on the screen.

Dammit.

"Answer it already." Chief trundled past them with another case in his arms. "We're pretty much done here, and your ring tone is driving me fucking batty."

Charlie pressed the answer button. "Hey, Dad, you always have such great timing." She glanced at Kellerman as he passed by her with his case, following Chief Ricard into the woods and heading toward the bus.

"Are you busy?" Captain Cutter had a knack for calling at all the wrong moments. When her boyfriend of three years had broken it of in college. When she'd received her first speeding ticket. When she decided to quit her master's degree program. Yes, his timing was impeccable.

Charlie scanned the empty beach. "Looks as if I'm free for a few minutes. What's up?" She took a seat on a flat rock about twenty yards from what little remained of the pod. She couldn't believe how quickly it had melted.

"Your mom wanted me to call. She's worried about you. The new job and all. How was your first day?"

It was as if their disagreement from the other day had never even happened. He'd always been this way. Brushing aside arguments as if nothing had gone wrong. Pretending as if everything was hunky-dory when it had really gone to shit. "Fine. My first day was fine. In fact, I'm still working."

"I'm sorry, Charlene."

Charlene. Again.

She tamped down her annoyance. Most people her age would be happy to have a parent call and ask about their first day of work. She, on the other hand, found it intrusive and overbearing. "Even if I were done for the day, I wouldn't have much to say. You know, security and all."

Her father worked at the NSA, which was a short drive from Washington Navy Yard. He had a clearance and knew the rules.

"Right. I understand that. Your mom had me call because I think she believes we can talk about work since we're both in the Navy. I didn't have the heart to explain it to her. You know how she is."

Charlie pictured her mother at home, prepping dinner for her father. Angela Cutter's main ambition in life had been to be a wife and mother. Now that Charlie and her brother were grown up and gone, her mother had turned her attentions to pampering her husband with elaborate home cooked meals and meddling in her children's lives. "Tell mom I'm doing fine. I'll give her a call tomorrow when things are calmer."

"Will do."

"Have you received your new orders yet?" He was due for a new assignment soon. He and her mother had been stationed at Fort Meade, Maryland for three years. Not a bad gig, really.

"Should hear from BUPERS any day."

"What are you hoping for?"

"Your mom would love to go overseas. Japan, I think. But I'd like to teach again. We'll see."

Demarco made his way toward her. He must've finished with his tests. Probably wouldn't look too good if she were chatting on her cell phone, which was now likely the property of NCIS-A, to have a chat with her dad. "I should go. I have more work to do."

"Sure, honey. I understand. I'm sorry for interrupting your day."

At the last moment, she realized she needed his help. "Dad, before you hang up, do you think when you get home tonight you could email me my research?"

"I thought you were done with that. In fact, I distinctly remember you telling me to drop your laptop off a cliff."

When she'd quit the graduate program at Baylor her research had hit a wall. She was not moving ahead as she'd anticipated at the beginning. Failure lurked around every corner and undermined her ability to decode the Voynich Manuscript. She'd not been used to failure. "I just need it, Dad. Could you email it, please?"

"If you were going to finish the research, why didn't you stick with it? Why did you give it up to enlist in the Navy?"

Same old issues. Time and again. "I'm not having this conversation now, Dad." Demarco was only twenty yards away. The last thing she needed was for him to hear her in a shouting match with her father. "Can't you do what I asked without any opinions or judgment thrown at me?"

"I could've gotten you an appointment to the Naval Academy, like Chad. I don't know why you always have to choose the hard way, Charlene."

"Charlie. I like to be called Charlie." Her voice rose higher than she intended. "How many times do I have to tell you that? Never mind about the files. I'll call Mom. She'll do it for me." She hung up and tossed the phone on the sand in front of her. Why did every conservation with him end up this way?

"Hope you don't mind if I keep calling you Cutter."

Demarco arrived at the most embarrassing point in her conversation. Great. "Cutter's fine." She huddled in her borrowed coat as the wind picked up.

"I'm going to have to take your phone now." Demarco picked it up and wiped off the sand. "Classified materials. I'll buy you a new one when we're somewhere less redneck."

Charlie smiled. Demarco could've made a bad situation worse, but he chose to spare her. "Is there anywhere less redneck in North Dakota?"

He held out a hand to help her up. "You've got a point. Maybe we'll wait 'til we return to D.C."

She accepted his assistance. "Unless you think Devils Lake has an Apple Store?" His hand was pleasantly warm, his grip sure.

He chuckled.

Yes, Charlie had actually made Mr. Tightass laugh. She considered her day a success.

They headed toward the woods to rejoin their group at the bus. Charlie looked forward to taking a hot shower and getting some sleep. It had been a very long day.

"Hey, help!" A cry came from the woods. "Cutter!"

Demarco took off before she could even react and plunged into the thicket.

The voice had sounded like Kellerman's. "We're coming!" Charlie raced toward her team member who needed her help.

———

Kellerman sat on the ground with his hand pressed to a bloody gash on his forehead. Ricard lay crumpled in a heap not much further away.

Demarco crouched over Ricard and tested the pulse in his neck. "What happened?" He directed his question at the young lieutenant.

Charlie pushed Kellerman's hand away from his wound. "Who hit you?" He had a good sized slice to his forehead. Possibly from a rock or a tree branch. There were plenty in the woods.

Kellerman shook off her ministrations and held his head in his hands. "Fuck, fuck, fuck!" He stood and scrounged for the remains of the case he'd been carrying. "He hit me over the head and took the samples."

Alarm rose up in Charlie. "What?"

Demarco focused back on the attack. "Who hit you? Where did he go?"

"Is Ricard okay?" Charlie couldn't think about the attacker. She had to deal with the situation in front of her first.

"Which way, Cole?" Demarco pulled a taser from his pocket.

Where the heck did that come from?

"Hey, where do you think you are going?" Charlie couldn't believe Demarco would dash off into the woods and leave two wounded co-workers behind. "You can't go running off by yourself. Let me help these guys make it back to Commander Orr, and I'll go with you."

"There's no time for that. Those samples are all we have. Someone must've been watching us the whole time."

Charlie took in the scene. Kellerman's case had been cracked open. All the test tubes she'd seen on the beach were gone. Ricard's case was missing entirely.

"I can take care of Ricard." Kellerman wiped the blood out of his eyes and made his way over to the unconscious chief. "You two go find the guy. Hurry."

Ricard moaned.

At least the chief was alive.

"Which way did he go?" Demarco asked.

"That way, I think." Kellerman pointed west into the woods along the lake.

"Fuck, Kellerman." Demarco stripped off his poncho. "We'd better find this guy or we're in a load of shit. Let's go, Cutter."

She nodded and paired up with Demarco. "Call the commander," she directed at Kellerman. "Let him know you guys need help out here."

She stuffed down her worries about Ricard's condition. She needed to be alert in order to help Demarco locate the person who'd attacked their people. Her mind flashed back to the strange footprints she'd seen earlier. Could it be that Demarco had been wrong about them? Maybe someone had been biding his time until he saw an opportunity to attack.

"Come on." Demarco plunged into the woods, his taser aimed straight ahead.

Charlie chased behind over limbs and downed trees, through scrubby bushes and underbrush. Minutes went by. Demarco pressed on.

The sun sat low in the sky. It would be dark soon. She hoped they could find some trace of the perpetrator before it was too late.

"Here. Look." Demarco pointed.

Ricard's case lay on its side. Test tubes had spilled out everywhere. All of them were smashed. As if someone had done it purposefully.

"See if you can salvage anything." Demarco indicated several indentations in the mossy ground and a broken tree branch. "See that? He went this way. I'll be right back."

"Wait. Give me my phone." Charlie held out her hand. "If you aren't back in ten minutes, I'm calling the Commander."

He pulled it out and handed it to her. "All right. Ten minutes."

When he hesitated, she shooed him away. "Go, go, go. I've got this. I'll pick up everything. You just get the bastard that did this."

Demarco nodded and disappeared into the darkening woods.

———

Charlie scooped up the remains of the test tubes. A little bit of green goo remained in several of them. With pincher fingers, she picked up each shard and placed it in the case. In the growing dark, it was hard to make out all the debris, but she worked methodically from the case outward. She had no other choice.

Maybe if they went back to the lake, they could still salvage more samples?

At the rate the pod had been deteriorating when she'd seen it last, that seemed unlikely. But maybe it was worth a shot. These samples were too important.

Her focus narrowed to the small patch of ground in front of her. The green substance could answer a lot of questions about what the pod was made of and where it might be from. Shouldn't Dr. Stern be able to tell the difference between a substance from earth and a substance from outer space?

She wished she had some gloves. She'd watched enough forensic specials on tv to know the way she was handling these small shards made DNA transfer unavoidable.

She glanced at her watch to keep track of the time. Only five minutes had passed since Demarco had continued on without her.

As she picked up every bit of glass she could find, she paused in her work and stood back for a better look at the scene to make sure she didn't miss anything. One larger piece of a test tube had fallen outside the range of her vision. It looked as if it might have some blood on it.

Blood.

From the person who'd attacked Kellerman and Ricard? This could be crucial evidence to save. She thought over the possibilities and took in her surroundings. Picking up a large maple leaf, damp and half decayed from last fall, she used it to carefully collect the shard. Wrapping it up in the leaf as best she could, she set it on top of the glass pieces already inside the case.

A crunch behind her made her freeze. The attacker had circled back for her. Her gut clenched.

"I lost him." Demarco emerged from the trees.

Thank God. Demarco.

The tense atmosphere lifted. No longer alone, she felt safer with the special agent there.

"I fucking lost him." He kicked at the base of a tree.

"What happened?"

"He vanished. I reached the edge of the woods on the other

side of the base, and the trail ended there. I don't understand.
We were right behind him. We had to be."

Demarco gripped the taser.

"You can put that away now," Charlie said quietly.

"Oh," He finally noticed he'd been pointing it toward her.
"Sorry." He tucked it in the back of his pants like a pistol. "This
whole day has been bizarre. I'm not thinking straight."

"That's okay." Charlie locked up the case. "I don't know
what's considered normal for this group. Glad to know you
think it's bizarre, too."

"We need to be on guard. I don't know where this guy's
gone." He scanned the forest around them. "He's willing to
attack two of our people, so he might try it again. Last thing I
need is for the newbie to end up hurt."

Charlie was rankled at the comment, but it wouldn't do her
any good to put up a fuss. Demarco had an issue with her, and
she had to learn how to work through it. Show him that she was
as useful and smart as anyone else on the team. Maybe then
he'd respect her.

"I collected as much as I could." She showed him the locked
case full of shards and bits of goo. "We should really join up
with the group. Find out more about what happened."

"Unlock your phone for me." Demarco handed it to her.

She held the phone in front of her face until it recognized
her image.

He dialed a number. "Commander Orr, it's Angel. Are
Kellerman and Ricard with you?"

Charlie shifted her attention to the sounds emerging from
the woods. The night creatures had awakened and strange
noises came at them from all directions. She longed to be back
in the safety of the bus, headed toward a motel room.

Demarco explained to the commander about the attack, the missing test tubes, and the unsuccessful chase.

Charlie wished they could keep walking. They'd done what they could. The perpetrator was gone. They weren't the cops. They didn't have CSI gear with them to track this person. Was this even related to the pod discovery? Or a random crime?

"We'll be there in ten." Demarco hung up and pocketed the phone.

"Kellerman and Ricard are okay. Someone from the National Guard depot has called for an ambulance. Ricard needs to be checked out, and Kellerman probably is going to need some stitches."

"Glad help is on the way."

"The commander said he was able to collect more samples from the pod. Stormy had an extra case. They might be more contaminated with lake water than the ones we had originally, but at least it's something."

"Maybe they can use what I was able to save." Charlie wished he'd pay a little more attention to her. It was as if he hadn't even been listening when she'd showed him the case she'd recovered. "I even found a shard with blood on it."

"You did?" Demarco had her full attention now. "Why didn't you tell me?"

"I did."

Demarco's jaw set in a line. "You never told me you had recovered any blood."

"You didn't ask." Charlie couldn't help but bite back. He was unpleasant, holier-than-thou, and condescending. The kindness of lending her his coat completely wore off. "I managed to recover some of the pod material plus a piece of glass with blood on it. It's all in the case."

Demarco snatched it from her. "Let me carry it. The last

thing we need is another mistake." He headed back in the direction of where they'd left Kellerman and Ricard.

Charlie fumed. How dare he judge her as a screw up. She'd done nothing to deserve that. Although she wanted to grab the case away from him and knock him over the head with it, she knew it would bite her in the ass and probably only prove him right in some way. She had to take the high road at this point and pick her battles with him. As this was only her first day, the last thing she needed to do was piss off her team.

While she tramped after him in the dark woods, she hoped tomorrow would be a better day. She looked forward to meeting back up with the rest of the team and reviewing the day's events and where they'd go from here. She also wanted a good look at the photos they'd taken. Once she received her Voynich research, she could start working on comparing the two. Maybe she could help figure out where this pod came from, if someone had been on it, and who had attacked them.

CHAPTER 9

CHARLIE AND DEMARCO emerged from the woods in time to witness an ambulance pulling away from the parking lot near the base commander's office. Orr, Lisa, and Kellerman stood in a huddle by their bus.

"Is Ricard going to be okay?" Demarco joined the small circle.

Charlie hung back. After one day with this group, she didn't know where she fit in yet. She was anxious to return to a secure office where she could review the photos, hopefully access her graduate school notes, and compare the writings on the pod to the Voynich writings. For now, though, she could only follow Demarco and the rest of the NCIS-A team around like a puppy dog and wait for orders.

"The EMTs seemed to think he'd be okay, but he needs to have an MRI to find out the extent of his injuries," Commander Orr said. "We don't fly out of here until tomorrow anyway, so it's probably a good idea for the chief to spend the night in the hospital. They'll transfer him to the Minot clinic in the morning."

Although Kellerman held a blood-soaked rag to his forehead, he seemed eager to talk to both Demarco and Charlie. "Did you find him? The guy who hit me and Chief?"

In the short time she'd gotten to know Kellerman, Charlie didn't think of him as an excitable kind of person. This attack, however, brought out the badger in him. "Demarco lost him on the other side of the base," she answered.

Demarco flashed her a hard stare.

Whoops. Guess the straight-laced special agent didn't like being called out when he failed to follow through.

"We tracked him through the woods, but he got away." Demarco opened up the circle for Charlie to join. "Maybe someone was waiting for him in a vehicle. That's the only explanation I can think of. We found your case."

He held up the case with the broken contents locked away inside.

Charlie could've punched him for claiming 'they' had found it together. "Do you have any tape? We need to seal it up. We have DNA inside."

"DNA?" Orr took the case. "What kind of DNA?"

"Blood. On one of the broken vials. There's also some tiny samples left from the pod."

"I managed to collect a few more samples." Lisa held another case similar to the one Charlie had recovered. "Not sure how pure they are, but I'm hoping Dr. Stern can do something with them."

"I might have enough for her to work with. We'll see." Charlie had many questions about this mysterious attacker that she wanted answered. "Who could've known what we were doing out here? I thought this was all top secret activity."

"There are plenty of people who could've found out about the pod from the farmer," Lisa said. "I read the report in there." She motioned toward the commandant's office where she and

Commander Orr had had their meeting while the rest of them were gathering their samples. "The guys on watch duty thought it was a meteor. Big, loud, flaming like a rocket engine. Enough to scare anyone that the end of the world had arrived. They met up with the farmer only a few minutes after he'd found it at the edge of the lake."

"The only reason the woods didn't set on fire was the rainstorm. Flooded most of the county," Commander Orr said. "We received the call only after it had been routed through Minot Air Force Base, which routed the call to NSA, which routed the call to our office. Plenty of people in the middle of all that could've sneaked out here to see what we were up to."

"You think they took any pictures or samples before we got here?" Charlie wondered if the mysterious attacker had arrived before they did and had taken better pictures of the writings.

"They sealed off the crash site immediately after impact." Demarco took out his taser and placed it back in its case, which sat on top of the other supplies they'd brought with them. "I doubt he would've made the move on Kellerman and the Chief, if he'd been able to collect his own samples. He stole the case, remember?"

"He destroyed it and the samples. If he wanted to keep them, he wouldn't have left them behind in the woods," Charlie pointed out. "Even according to you, the guy was long gone before we ever started tracking him. If he'd been interested in the samples, he could've gotten away with it easily. Instead he broke all the vials, cutting himself in the process."

"Good point, Petty Officer Cutter." Commander Orr clapped her on the shoulder. "Very astute observation. In other words, this person came here to sabotage our investigation."

Demarco's face darkened.

"Thanks, Commander." The more she thought about the

events of the day, the more it made sense to her. The footprints in the sand, the chase down the beach...someone had done that to draw them away from the pod and away from the samples and pictures they'd been collecting. Four against one would've made the odds very bad for someone looking to destroy any evidence of the pod. But with her and Demarco at the other end of the beach, it would've been much easier for a lone attacker to take down Kellerman and Chief.

"Who would have reason to do something like this?" Lisa asked. She'd already packed up both cases, carefully sealing the recovered case with yellow tape to ensure the blood evidence remained intact and untouched until they returned to D.C.

"Conspiracy theorists, militia groups, you name it," Demarco said. "There's always someone who believes the government is inherently bad and wants to keep secrets from the American public."

"But aren't we keeping secrets from the American public?" Charlie asked.

"Yes, but part of the job of the government is to protect its citizens." Orr locked a stack of file folders in a box. He lowered his voice. "Until we know what these pods are, where they come from, and if they are extraterrestrial, it's our job to keep this a secret."

"It's been a long day," Lisa interjected. "We collected a lot of data, and it's going to take time for us to dig through it all. Why don't we save the theories for another day, shall we? The guy ran away, but he didn't take anything. We're not going to figure this out right now." She grabbed the two sample cases and loaded them in the secure storage area under the bus. "I'd like to find our motel and take a shower, if that's okay with everyone else."

Demarco aided Lisa with the task of loading their equipment. Kellerman boarded the bus, with his head wound unbandaged.

Commander Orr drew Charlie aside. "I know this hasn't been easy for you. There's a lot you still need to learn about our office, our job, and what's expected of you."

Charlie wanted to unload how she felt about her first day on the job, but sensed the timing was wrong. "I'm trying to play catch up as best I can."

"You need to trust me. When we're out on site like this, we can't be as open as we would like." Orr scanned the parking lot around them. "We have to do our best to follow security protocols. There will be a time and a place for us to discuss our work more freely. Have patience."

Charlie nodded. She'd only recently received her clearance and should've known better than to broadcast their activities in such a public setting.

"Why don't you board the bus with Kellerman? We'll finish loading everything."

"I'm sorry, Commander."

"Don't be sorry, Petty Officer. We need you on our team. Don't you ever doubt that."

———

Charlie swiped the key card through the door lock at Devils Lake Motel and entered her room—two queen beds covered with depressing brown comforters, a small fridge, and a flat screen tv. Not bad for middle-of-nowhere North Dakota.

She shivered. The maid must've left the air conditioning on all day even though it had been less than warm at the lake. She kicked herself for handing Demarco back his trench coat when they'd exited the bus.

Charlie adjusted the thermostat and picked up the motel directory. Even though night had fallen by the time they'd arrived at the motel, she hoped a store was within walking distance that carried toiletries.

As she flipped through the meager business offerings of Devils Lake, she glanced out the window. Across the street a gas station with a mini mart still had its lights on. Worth a shot.

She put her key card in her skirt pocket and hoped her room would warm up before she returned from her errands.

The Devils Lake Motel was located a few blocks from Highway 2. The town appeared deserted. No cars were visible on the road. The only sound was the loud scratchy rhythm of cicadas.

When she entered the mini mart, the female clerk glanced up from the romance novel she was reading. "We close in ten minutes." Her greasy brown hair had been pulled back from her shiny, pimply face with a pink rubber band. The clerk scanned Charlie from head to toe. Probably wasn't typical for someone in a Navy uniform to stroll in the door.

Charlie glanced at her watch. Almost nine o'clock. "I should be quick." She searched the short aisles for anything useful picking up toothpaste, a toothbrush, a comb, a small round brush, a bottle of hairspray, and deodorant. At the back of the store she spied T-shirts and sweatshirts with 'Devils Lake' on them. She grabbed one of each and a pair of sweatpants.

"Do you have any of those disposable cell phones?" Behind the counter, Charlie saw minute cards for sale for a variety of pay-as-you-go cell phone plans.

The girl got up from her stool and grabbed a flip phone package from the case near the lottery tickets. "This is all we got."

"I'll take it." Charlie dumped the rest of her items on the counter.

The girl took her time scanning each item. The sweatshirt, T-shirt, and pants had to be punched in separately. As Charlie waited to pay, she glanced out the plate glass window. A figure lurked near their bus. It was too dark and too far away for her to determine if it was someone from their team.

"Cash or credit?"

Charlie fished her wallet out of her purse and handed the clerk her credit card. She returned her gaze to the bus. At that very moment, an eighteen-wheeler blew by, obscuring her view. By the time the truck passed, the figure had vanished.

"You put it in the machine yourself." The clerk pointed at the reader on the counter.

"Sorry." She put her card in the chip reader slot. "Thanks."

The clerk handed her a bag and a receipt. Then she picked up her romance novel.

The bell on the door jangled.

"We're closing, sir." The clerk set her book down for a second time.

Charlie looked over her shoulder at the new customer.

Kellerman had entered. He seemed surprised to see Charlie. "Hey."

"Hey." Charlie smiled. He must've been the figure out by the bus.

"Thought you'd be dead asleep by now."

"That's a nasty gash there." The last time she'd seen Kellerman he'd been holding a rag to his forehead. The jagged cut oozed fresh blood.

Kellerman reached up to touch the wound. "Thought I'd see if they had any bandages. Didn't want to mess up the motel towels."

"First Aid. Aisle Two." The clerk, her nose deep in her book, pointed to the correct aisle. "I gotta close up soon."

Kellerman and Charlie searched the aisle for the right sized bandages.

"Do you like Spiderman?" Charlie held up the two boxes available. "Or Hello Kitty?"

"How about some gauze and tape instead?" Kellerman grabbed a box of gauze off the shelf.

Charlie imagined computer nerd Kellerman with Hello Kitty bandages stuck across his forehead and smiled. "You have something against Hello Kitty?"

Kellerman laughed. "My brother would kick my ass if he thought I was even considering it. He caught me playing Barbies with my little sister once and told all of my friends. I was a pariah at school for a month. He still brings it up at Thanksgiving."

Charlie returned the boxes to the shelf. "I would've kept your secret."

"But Demarco wouldn't."

Charlie saw an opportunity to suss out more details about her co-worker. "What is his problem, by the way?"

"Demarco?" Kellerman carried his gauze and tape to the counter.

"Yeah. Does he have a problem with me or is it all women?"

The clerk rang up the purchases.

Kellerman handed the woman a ten dollar bill. "Demarco's hard core, that's all."

"Hard core jack-ass?"

Kellerman didn't bite. "Deep down he's a good guy."

"Could've fooled me."

"He doesn't trust you yet."

They both exited the mini mart and headed back to the

motel. The clerk snapped off the outside lights as soon as they left. Guess she wanted to make sure no more last minute customers ruined her evening.

Charlie thought about Kellerman's explanation as they crossed the street. She was new to the team, true. She understood that. Guess she'd have to prove to Demarco that not only was she trustworthy, but that she brought some skills.

They'd reached the bus in the parking lot. The locked storage section under the bus was wide open.

"Shit!" Kellerman exclaimed.

Charlie instantly thought of the figure she'd seen outside the bus moments before Kellerman had appeared in the mini mart. If it hadn't been Kellerman, who had she seen? And what had they taken?

Kellerman pawed through the boxes and bins that were stored inside the locked bus compartment.

Charlie held back. There wasn't room for two of them under there. "Is anything missing?"

"I'm not sure." He checked the locks on all the secure boxes. "I didn't help load it."

Charlie spied one of the sample boxes still inside the storage compartment. But where was the box with the yellow tape? The one with the blood sample inside? "The other sample box is missing. I don't see it."

Kellerman moved more quickly after that revelation. "Are you sure it wasn't put in one of the equipment boxes?"

Most of the items had been stowed inside large metal boxes with keyed locks. "I'm certain. Besides, the other box is right there." Charlie pushed past Kellerman and scooped up the remaining sample box.

Who had left the samples unprotected and sitting inside the compartment?

"Dammit." Kellerman sat back on his heels. "What the hell is going on? The commander needs to see this."

Charlie pulled out her brand new cell phone, still in the package and inactive. "You can use this."

He glanced at the uncharged, most likely unusable phone. "Go find the commander. I think he's in room 216."

Charlie hesitated. "Will you be okay alone out here?" She wanted to tell Kellerman she'd seen someone out in the parking lot earlier, but something made her pause. It had been interesting that Kellerman had appeared in the mini mart only minutes after Charlie had seen a shadowy figure hanging out near the bus.

"Just go." Kellerman closed the compartment door. "Someone broke the lock. Shit."

"I'll be back in a minute. Don't worry." Charlie trotted toward the motel lobby entrance. "Commander Orr will fix this." She said that last sentence mostly to herself. Even though she'd only met him that morning, she trusted Orr. He exuded some of the same characteristics as her father—serious, unflappable, tough. She would tell him what she saw in the parking lot moments before the break-in discovery.

The hotel desk clerk, an older woman with gray-streaked hair and orange lipstick, greeted her. "How are you this evening?"

Before heading up to Orr's room, Charlie had a thought. "Do you have a security camera in your parking lot?"

The woman nodded. "Put one in three years ago after the Elks Club convention."

Charlie sensed the clerk wanted her to ask about the convention, but she was in no mood to chat. "Please make sure you keep tonight's video. We had a break in."

"I'm so sorry." The clerk tapped her fingernails in a nervous rhythm on the counter. "I should probably call the night manager. He should be here by nine-thirty. Do you want me to call him?"

"My boss will probably want to talk to him. Maybe give him a heads up." Charlie grabbed a pad of motel note paper and a pen that sat on the counter. "What's his name?"

"Merle. He's been the night manager here for fifteen years."

Charlie scribbled his name on the paper. "Thanks." She ripped the top paper off the pad and shoved it in her pocket.

"No problem, honey. Sorry about the break-in. I didn't see anything, and I've been here since seven." The clerk pointed at the clock above the entrance.

Charlie headed for the stairs at the end of the first floor wing of rooms. She took the stairs two at a time, stopped in front of room 216, and knocked. God, she hoped Commander Orr wasn't too upset. What if the blood evidence she'd collected was now in the hands of an enemy?

The door swung open to reveal Special Agent Angel Demarco in a towel.

Charlie's face grew hot at the sight of his well-sculpted bare chest, muscular arms, and the thin material wrapped around his waist that left very little to the imagination. Damn Kellerman for giving her the wrong room number. She should've asked the desk clerk to double check for her before she bolted upstairs.

"Cutter, what in the hell are you doing here?" Demarco didn't seem pleased but did nothing to cover up.

"Kellerman told me this was Commander Orr's room." She sputtered and averted her eyes. Better to focus on Demarco's face. "Someone broke into the bus storage compartment. Do you know what room he's in?"

"What? Come in here." Demarco grabbed her and pulled her into his room. The door shut with a slam.

Charlie yanked her arm free. "I need to talk to the commander."

"Slow down, Cutter. Slow down." Demarco rubbed his wet hair with an extra towel. "Sit."

Although she wanted to bolt out of the room and find the Commander, she found herself following the special agent's commands. The tone of his voice made her obey rather than leave. She hoped Kellerman was okay alone in the parking lot. "We need help. The desk clerk has video. Maybe we can find out who did this." She took a seat on one of the two queen-sized beds in the room and put her bag of clothing and toiletries in her lap.

"What were you doing in the parking lot?" Demarco grabbed a pair of pajama pants out of his duffel bag and headed for the bathroom.

Of course the jerk would find something wrong with her story. "I went across the street to the mini mart...look, why I was out there has nothing to do with what happened."

Demarco disappeared into the bathroom, but left the door partially open so they could continue their conversation. "Did you see anything? You said Kellerman was there with you."

Charlie knew Kellerman was waiting for her. This delay was ridiculous. By the time she was done answering Demarco's questions, the perpetrator would be long gone. "When I was across the street I thought I saw someone by the bus. I couldn't make him out. Then, later when we crossed the street—"

"Kellerman went to the mini mart with you?"

She wanted to kick the man in the shins. "He showed up after I got there. Do you want to hear the rest of this or not? I really need to talk to the commander. Do you not understand how important that is?"

Demarco came out of the bathroom more suitably dressed in a pair of plaid pajamas, but no shirt. It was as if he enjoyed making her uncomfortable. "You saw someone by the bus. Kellerman shows up. You both cross the street and—?"

"That's when we noticed the storage compartment had been broken into."

"Anything missing?"

"The sample box we taped closed. I didn't see it in there."

Demarco raised an eyebrow. Finally, some kind of normal reaction out of the man.

"What room is the commander in?" Charlie demanded. "We need to start an investigation. Retrieve the video footage. Call the police. Shut down the town. Whatever we have to do to get that evidence back."

"We can track it." Demarco sat on the other bed and cracked open his laptop.

"What?"

"I put air tags on both sample boxes—is that what you call them? Give me one minute, and I can tell you the exact longitude and latitude of their location."

Thank God for technology. Maybe Demarco could find it. "What about Kellerman?" Charlie wondered what the computer geek thought of her prolonged absence. She needed to get back to him.

"Hold on." Demarco opened up an application. "I have to find the item in the list, hit 'search,' and let the computer do the rest." He worked the touchpad with his forefinger and scrolled to the correct item.

If they found the box, they would likely find the person who stole it. Would it would turn out to be the same person they'd chased through the woods earlier that day? Maybe the mysterious attacker didn't want them to have a sample of his blood or the pod or both.

"Got it." A crooked smile appeared on his face. "Stormy gave me an inservice on these little things. Really handy. She uses them all the time on her kids' backpacks. Here you go." He turned around his laptop so she could see the map on his screen. A little green dot flashed.

Charlie took in the information. The dot was located in their motel. "The box is here?"

"Looks like it." Demarco turned the computer back in his direction. "I should be able to narrow down the range, if I can remember how to do it."

"Can you figure out what room?"

"Give me a second." He tapped on his keyboard. "It's across the hall." Demarco looked up and his gaze burned into her. "Kellerman's room."

CHAPTER 10

DEMARCO OPENED up the nightstand drawer and pulled out his taser.

"What are you doing?" Charlie couldn't imagine Kellerman as the thief. Yes, it seemed suspicious that he'd appeared in the mini mart only a few minutes after she'd spied someone lurking around the bus, but he'd been attacked only hours earlier in the woods. Was Demarco suggesting by his actions that Kellerman had injured himself to cover his tracks?

"You can stay here." Demarco set the taser on the bed and put on a T-shirt. "I'll take care of this." His brown gaze hardened.

Charlie grabbed the taser and backed up. "This is crazy. You can't believe it's Kellerman."

Demarco took a few measured steps toward her. "Give me back the taser, Charlie."

It was the first time he hadn't called her 'Cutter.' She reached for the doorknob. "No. This is ridiculous. You're jumping to conclusions."

"He hasn't been in the office very long. Not much longer than you, actually." He leveled his gaze at her. "The work we do is too important to screw up. We aren't about to get this close to finding some real evidence, some tangible proof of alien life, only to have a weasel like Kellerman run back to Nevada with it. Give me the taser."

"No. I won't. I'm not going anywhere until you get Commander Orr in here." She thought about her options. Dash into the bathroom and lock herself in? Head out into the hallway and bang on Kellerman's door?

The bathroom would be a dead end. Demarco could easily bash in the door. If she ran into the hallway, Demarco would be seconds behind her if she tried to grab Kellerman's attention. She only had one option if Demarco refused her command. Charlie pointed the taser directly at his chest. "Don't come any closer."

Demarco raised his hands. "Whoa, hey, slow down. You don't want to hurt someone with that thing."

"I won't, if you do as I ask." Charlie willed herself to remain calm. She had no clue how to operate a taser, but if she had to, she'd figure it out. It looked enough like her father's .45. "Get Commander Orr in here."

He took a step backward toward the bed. "We're going to lose that case. Is that what you want?" His gaze darted over at the open laptop. "The box is on the move." His whole body tensed. "We have to go."

Charlie kept the taser steadily aimed at Demarco's torso. "Shut up. Call Orr. I want to talk to him." She didn't know why she trusted Orr more than she trusted Demarco, but since the special agent acted so irrationally when confronted with the missing box, she had to rely on someone. Orr had the authority to put Demarco in his place until they sorted this whole thing out.

Demarco's face turned red. "Fuck, fuck, fuck." He picked

up the phone and dialed. He stared at her. "You don't know what you're doing, Cutter."

"Just get Orr." Charlie willed her hand to be still. She'd never done this before. Threatening someone with a weapon was outside her realm of experience. She was riding on instinct alone. "If Kellerman really does have the box, the tracker will show us exactly where he is." Maybe that would calm him down. No need to panic if the box could be found at a moment's notice.

"Commander, sorry I'm bothering you so late. I have a situation in my room." Demarco gave her a hard look. "Cutter's lost her mind. Could you please come here?"

He hung up before Charlie could complain about his choice of words. She regripped the taser in her sweaty hand. "Don't try anything stupid."

"What do you think I'd try to do to you? Kellerman's probably gone already. I don't have any beef with you. Put it down. You look ridiculous."

Each second that ticked by Charlie doubted herself a little bit more. Did she make the wrong choice? Did she just find herself out of a job?

Someone knocked on the door. "Angel, what's going on?"

Charlie backed up with the taser still pointed at Demarco. Now that she'd set on that course of action, she felt she had to stick to it. Even if she was losing trust in her own judgment. She felt for the doorknob and opened the door. "Come in, Commander."

Orr stepped into the room. "What in the hell is going on here?"

"She's crazy." Demarco didn't waste any time. "Thanks for adding such a valued new member to the team."

Charlie didn't appreciate the sarcasm. "Commander, there

is something weird going on, and I don't know what to make of it."

"And that requires you pointing a taser at Demarco? I don't recall you being qualified in that particular weapon." The commander easily plucked the taser from her sweaty fingers. "There'd better be a good explanation for this, Petty Officer."

Orr made her feel like a little kid with that move. If they'd only listen to her for a minute, they might actually get somewhere.

Demarco relaxed, leaning back against the headboard. "Yes, explain it to him, Cutter. I'm sure he'd love to hear your theories."

"It isn't a theory." Charlie knew Demarco would never take her side on this. Orr was the key. "Kellerman didn't take that box."

"What box?" Commander Orr directed his question at Demarco.

Charlie answered it before the special agent had a chance to take over. "The box we'd sealed at the crash site with the blood evidence of the attacker. Demarco seems to think Kellerman stole it."

"A box was stolen from our secure compartment?" Orr tensed. "Why didn't anyone tell me?"

Charlie didn't have time to explain more. Someone had the case. They needed to find out who. "There's a tracker device on the box. See?" She turned Demarco's laptop to show her boss the blip on the screen. The screen was blank. "What the hell? Where's the tracker?"

Demarco gave a tight smile. "I told you we needed to move. Kellerman's probably miles down the road. There'll be a refresh in a minute." He tapped on the touch pad to update the information.

"Kellerman stole the evidence?" Orr handed the taser back to Demarco. "He was thoroughly vetted before we offered him a spot on the team. He has a top secret clearance. There were no connections in his background to any organizations or foreign governments. I can't believe he would betray us like this. What motive could he possibly have?"

Charlie watched as the tracker data updated. "It's still in his room. Let's go ask him."

She headed for the door before either of the two men could respond. In a moment she stood outside Kellerman's door.

At her knock, the door opened.

"Where have you been?" Kellerman stood in the doorway, the sealed box in his hands. "I found it."

Charlie grabbed the box from him and checked the tape seals. "Where was it?"

Demarco and Orr caught up to her moments later.

"Hey, Commander." Kellerman greeted his superior and opened the door to let everyone inside. "Am I glad to see you."

No mention was made of their earlier suspicions. Charlie knew Demarco didn't want to admit he'd rushed to judgment in front of her.

"Lieutenant," Orr greeted the junior officer. "Cutter told us about the break in."

"Don't worry, I managed to relock the compartment. Stormy's standing guard for now."

Demarco took the box out of Charlie's hands. "Where did you find this? Cutter told us it was missing."

"I thought it was, too. But we were wrong. It was buried under the other boxes. We overreacted."

Charlie could feel the heat of a blush flood her cheeks. She had been positive the box wasn't in the compartment. They'd looked through the whole space. That yellow tape would've stuck out like a full moon on a starless night.

Kellerman continued his story, "After Petty Officer Cutter went looking for you, Commander, I called Stormy, and we did a thorough inventory. All items on the list were accounted for. Once I pulled everything out, I found the sealed box."

"Why would someone break in and not steal anything?" Charlie needed more of an explanation. Although she trusted Kellerman, something wasn't right with the scenario. "It doesn't make sense."

"Agreed." Commander Orr nodded. "Has anyone bothered to find out if the motel has video of the parking lot?"

"Yes." Charlie glanced at Demarco, waiting for an objection. "The front desk clerk told me they have a camera out front and that the night manager should be able to give us the footage."

Orr took control. "Demarco, go talk to the night manager about the footage."

Charlie deflated. The video had been her idea.

"Lieutenant, you are in charge of the box." Orr opened up the closet by the bathroom to reveal a safe embedded in the wall. "It should fit in there."

"Yes, sir." Kellerman took possession.

"And what about me, sir?" Charlie asked. In a room full of testosterone, she felt oddly unnecessary.

"You and I will take turns standing watch at the bus. I'll take the next shift. You relieve me at 0200."

The clock on the nightstand read ten o'clock. Her turn was four hours away. Even though the commander probably expected her to sleep, she had other ideas.

Everyone left Kellerman's room for their assigned duties. Charlie headed in the direction of her room, but once the hallway was empty, she took the stairs back to the lobby. If she didn't insert herself into the investigation, she'd always be an outsider in the office. She'd pulled a taser on a superior, which could end her career if she didn't get ahead of things. The security camera had been her idea. She should be involved in what clues they could glean from its footage.

————

At the bottom of the stairs, Charlie quietly opened the door. From her vantage point she could see the special agent leaning over the counter, smiling and talking to a middle aged man in a golf shirt and a pair of khaki pants. Looked like the clerk she'd spoken with earlier had ended her shift. This must be the night manager, Merle.

She was too far away to hear their conversation, but if she stepped any closer she might be seen.

Screw it.

Why did she care if Demarco saw her anyway? He already thought she was an idiot. How much lower could his opinion of her go?

She boldly stepped into the lobby. "Are you Merle?"

The man behind the counter looked up and gave her a smile. "That's me." He was missing a front tooth and, on closer inspection, Merle looked to be in his late thirties. A decade or two of hard drinking and cigarettes probably prematurely aged the man and gave him the smidgen of a potbelly that puffed out his shirt.

"You were supposed to be resting," Demarco ground out.

Charlie ignored him. "I asked your clerk to save tonight's footage from the parking lot. Can we take a look at it?"

Demarco had his NCIS badge laid out on the counter. Its

shiny gold shield glinted in the overhead lights. "The camera's down. There's no footage to view."

Her heart sank. This was going to be her moment. The moment she graduated from being the newbie in the office with zero experience to possibly being the helpful newbie in the office with some sleuthing skills. "Are you serious?" Her adolescent whine sounded ridiculous to her own ears.

Merle frowned. "I don't know why Donna told you it was working. When the storm hit, we lost power for a few hours. When the electricity came back on, the power surged and blew the computer in the back. We gotta buy a replacement before we're up and running again."

"Give it up, Cutter. We don't have anything." Demarco stuffed his badge into his pajama pants pocket. His damp, black hair curled slightly around his ears. "If you're going to stand watch later tonight, you need to rest."

"Sorry guys." Merle shrugged. "Wish I could help."

Once again she'd failed.

Demarco must've noticed her dejected appearance. "It's okay. Like Kellerman said, whoever broke in didn't take anything important." His gentleness surprised her.

"Yes, that's the good news."

"We should probably double check Stormy's inventory in the morning, though," said Demarco. "I had trackers on the secured things."

They headed back to the elevators. The adrenaline that had been keeping her going had worn off. Exhaustion settled in. She'd been in D.C. that morning, and now she was in Timbuktu, North Dakota. Demarco was right. She'd better sleep, or she'd be nonfunctional soon. "I'm glad to hear that."

Demarco reached to press the elevator call button at the same time she did. Their hands touched. Charlie yanked hers back as if burned. Demarco grinned, but said nothing and pressed the 'up' button.

Charlie cringed at her childish reaction. Time to change the subject. "Have you heard anything about Chief?"

They stepped inside the empty elevator.

"I'm sure the commander will update us when he knows anything. We have Camp Grafton on high alert." Demarco pressed the second floor button. "They're doing twenty-four hour guards at all entrances and keeping records of all vehicles coming and going until we figure out who attacked him."

"Don't you think he's long gone by now?"

"Maybe." The elevator opened, and he ushered her out first. "But our blood evidence may give us some more data to work with, so we'll want to keep track of everything. It's all about the details."

They shared the quiet corridor for a few moments. Charlie paused in front of her room before unlocking it. Without clearing the air between them, she'd have trouble sleeping. "I wanted to apologize for earlier...the taser." Admitting weakness was not something she liked to do, but in this case, if she wanted to be accepted at her new job, she needed to learn humility.

The special agent leaned against the wall and crossed his arms. "You haven't used one of those things before, have you?"

"Was it that obvious?" She slid her key card through the door lock.

"Maybe." He waited as she opened her door.

"Guess I'll see you in the morning." She flipped the light on in her room.

Angel Demarco lingered.

What was he waiting for?

"Be careful on watch tonight." The commanding tone his

voice usually held was gone. "You remember how to shoot a .45?"

All Navy shipmates were trained on how to operate and shoot a .45 pistol in Boot Camp. He knew that. "Of course."

"Good." The special agent's tone shifted. "Might come in handy. Good night." Demarco pushed off of the wall and headed down the hall toward his room.

As the door closed behind her, Charlie checked her watch. Eleven o'clock. She should be able to catch a couple hours' sleep before her two o'clock shift. She set her watch to go off at one a.m., with a second alarm set for one-thirty, if she slept through the first one. She glanced at the desk and zoned in on the coffee maker. A few cups of coffee shouldn't take much time to prepare. She'd done plenty of night watches at DLI. This would be no different.

Her energy level crashed after so much adrenaline. She kicked off her shoes, flopped onto the bed fully clothed, wrapped up in the comforter, and fell into a deep sleep.

———

Charlie's alarm blared. Six-thirty a.m. Her eyelids drooped. Out of coffee, since she'd drunk it all last night to prep for her four hours of uneventful watch duty, she stumbled into the bathroom and tossed cold water on her face. A short cat nap after her watch had only made her more tired. Their bus would be leaving in thirty minutes. She shrugged out of her wrinkled clothes and hopped into a tepid shower.

Their plane would be leaving Minot at ten. She hoped Chief would be able to make the flight. She hadn't heard an update on his condition since he'd been wheeled into the ambulance.

Someone knocked on her door.

Dammit.

She turned off the shower, grabbed a towel, and wrapped it around her. "Who is it?" Soapy water dripped down her legs. She shivered on the bath mat.

"You all packed up?" Lisa asked on the other side of her door. "I'm here to make sure your stuff is loaded on the bus."

"I don't have any luggage. I'm good." She barely had a toothbrush with her. She'd be walking out of the motel with only her purse and a caffeine headache.

"Oh, I forgot. Breakfast is down in the lobby whenever you're ready. Bus is out of here at oh-seven-hundred."

"Gotcha." Charlie rubbed her hair dry with an extra towel she pulled off the rack above the toilet. She had no make-up, no styling tools. Back to Boot Camp basics. Thank God the motel provided a blow dryer.

She reluctantly pulled on the sweatshirt and sweatpants she'd purchased the night before—baggy but comfortable. They'd be back in D.C. later today, and she could return to her temporary quarters at the base motel. She'd arrived at her new assignment location with two full suitcases and nothing else. The Navy would be delivering her shipped items in a couple of weeks. But at least she had fresh clothes and toiletries waiting for her once she returned.

She dried her hair and grimaced at the straight ends that flipped up every which way around her head. She should've asked Lisa if she had a straightening iron she could borrow. Her shoulder-length hair was barely long enough to put up in a braid. Without more styling tools at her fingertips, it didn't want to obey her desires.

Ugh.

She leaned toward the mirror. Without any mascara or

lipstick, she looked like a twelve-year-old. Her nickname in Boot Camp had been 'Kiddie Cutter.' She'd hated that nickname. Her Recruit Division Commander or RDC had coined that term her first day at Great Lakes. Who knows why. She wasn't the only girl who'd appeared younger than her age when all the make-up and hair styling was stripped away. But for some reason, her RDC had flagged her for teasing almost immediately.

After nine weeks in Boot Camp, she'd been glad to leave behind the name. Not many graduates were headed to DLI. Only a handful were on the plane with her. None of them had been in her unit. 'Kiddie Cutter' disappeared into her past. But this morning, she faced it once again.

Demarco would likely be one who would notice and find a way to use it against her. She braced for the reaction he'd have to her innocent appearance.

She checked her watch. Ten minutes to seven. She'd need to rush if she wanted anything to eat.

She grabbed her purse, stuffed her wrinkled uniform items into a bag, left her key on the bureau with a three dollar tip for the maid, and headed out the door.

Commander Orr joined her in the hall. "Get much sleep, Cutter?"

Thank goodness he didn't comment on her appearance or her clothes. "A bit. What about you?" The commander appeared identical to yesterday: pressed clothes, shiny shoes, hair combed perfectly. He probably never felt out of sorts. He didn't seem like the type who would leave unprepared for the unexpected.

He shrugged. "I can sleep on the plane."

"True. I was just glad that my shift was uneventful."

They stepped into the elevator together.

"I hear that. I'll feel better when we have everything packed up and back in the office. We have a lot of evidence to sort through, pictures to upload to the database, notes to transcribe."

He left off the particulars of the evidence. She knew why. Speaking openly about classified topics was verboten. Only within the walls of a SCIF—Sensitive Compartmented Information Facility—would it be safe to discuss all the details of their trip and what transpired.

"Dr. Stern will be happy to finally have some solid samples to work from." The elevator door opened to the lobby and Commander Orr waited, letting Charlie exit first.

"I've heard a few people mention Dr. Stern." She'd filed the name away for later. Now seemed like the perfect time to find out more about the absent member of the NCIS-A team. "Why didn't she come with us?"

Her boss led her to the buffet line where her co-workers milled around the tables selecting breakfast items. "Dr. Stern doesn't work for us exclusively. We only use her time when our investigations pan out. I'm sure you'll meet her when we return. She was hoping for great samples this trip. I'm sure with you on the team, you and Dr. Stern can work together on the photos."

Charlie nodded. They'd have time later to discuss further the details of those photos. She was eager to dig into the mysterious symbols and compare them to her graduate research. Maybe she'd even have an opportunity on the plane. She hadn't looked at her graduate work in long time. It might be good to refresh herself on where she'd left things before she'd abandoned her studies and joined the Navy.

"I have a seat for you over here, Charlene." Lisa waved at her from across the lobby.

Charlie wanted to correct her new friend on her preferred nickname, but decided now was not the time to fuss. She grabbed a mug, filled it with coffee, and piled a plate with fresh fruit, a bagel, and cream cheese. She smiled at Lisa and made her way over to the table.

"You look different." Demarco said as she passed his table. He sat with Kellerman near a window facing the parking lot. "When they said they were sending us a newbie, I had no idea how new."

Instead of taking on his slight, she ignored him and continued on her way.

"Leave her alone," Kellerman said.

Charlie warmed at the defense. Kellerman might be a nerd, but at least he was a gentleman.

CHAPTER 11

CHARLIE SMILED at Kellerman and joined Stormy at a table.

"Interesting outfit," her co-worker pointed out, a grin on her face.

"They didn't have much available in my size at the gas station across the street."

"Sorry your first day had to be so crazy. Next time you'll be ready with a go-bag at work. We're used to last minute assignments."

"This is normal? I thought A Group had only been around for a year or so?"

Her features dimmed. "Not here." Stormy nodded in the direction of Merle who was wrapping up his night shift by serving breakfast to guests.

Charlie had a lot she wanted to ask, but work with a security clearance had its problems. They'd have to wait until they were in a secure environment before openly talking about anything related to A Group. "Oh, sorry." She focused on her bagel and fruit.

"No harm. No foul." The two women ate in silence and

watched as the men from their team went for seconds at the buffet.

"We're out of here in five, folks." Commander Orr dumped his empty paper plate in the garbage and set his mug in the self-busing area.

Only a few other motel guests were eating breakfast that early in the day, so they had the room mostly to themselves.

Kellerman smiled and nodded as he passed them both with an empty tray and headed out to the parking lot. Orr and Demarco stood near the floor-to-ceiling window that looked out over an overgrown lawn. The front end of their bus was visible to the far left.

Although the two men were engaged in deep conversation, the arrival of more guests created loud chatter, which drowned out anything she might've been able to overhear.

Last night had been strange, and she didn't yet trust Kellerman or Demarco. Something about what she'd witnessed didn't make any sense. She glanced at Stormy. Would the older petty officer be someone she could share her thoughts with? For now she felt removed from her team, as if she were a stranger in her new assignment.

"Come on," said Stormy, picking up her tray. "Let's get out of here."

Gladly, Charlie glommed onto the woman. Lisa Storm had been the kindest of them all, so she wanted to make every effort to be kind in return.

"Do you have any family?" Stormy asked as she dumped her breakfast garbage into the bin.

"Yes." The question caught her off guard. "I've got a brother, Chad. And my parents. What about you?"

"So you're not married?" She scanned Charlie from head to toe.

The sweatsuit probably made her think Charlie wasn't exactly a catch. Her face grew hot. "No."

Stormy nodded. "Well, no rush, you're young."

"Maybe someday down the road," she said. To her, a husband and children were more than 'down the road,' they were miles and miles away, and she had plenty of road to travel alone until she reached them.

They made their way amicably out the front door. The bus's engine rumbled as it idled in the lot.

Charlie spied Orr and Demarco still inside talking near the window. If it wasn't a public place, she would've suspected they were conferring about their trip to Devils Lake and last night's break in. But as Stormy had pointed out, talking about classified topics outside of a SCIF wouldn't be allowed.

Demarco looked out, and his eyes locked with hers. A wave of goose bumps ran over her flesh. Charlie quickly averted her gaze. How mortifying he'd caught her staring.

"Stay away from that one," Stormy warned.

She swallowed. Her new work friend had seen the exchange between her and Demarco. "Oh?"

As her co-worker boarded the bus, she explained, "He's got a sordid history with a lot of women on base."

Instead of asking Stormy to clarify what 'a lot' meant, Charlie followed her on board. But she had a hard time forgetting the way her body flushed and her heart raced when his gaze had caught hers.

———

Charlie strapped herself into one of the jump seats and geared up for the flight home. Everyone was aboard with the exception of Chief Ricard who had to stay overnight at the hospital due to his head injury.

Now that they'd completed the information gathering portion of their investigation, she was eager to do her part— compare the Voynich Manuscript to the photos she snapped on her now secured cell phone.

As the pilot taxied down the runway at Minot, the Russian national anthem echoed through the fuselage.

Orr stood and maneuvered to the origin of the noise using the seat backs and hanging straps to steady his movements. He reached the cases with their evidentiary materials.

"It's my phone, sir," said Charlie.

"I gathered as much," he said and unlocked the case with a key he had on a lanyard around his neck. "Someone forgot to turn it off when it was placed in the case."

Orr gave a hard stare at the whole team.

Kellerman had his headphones on with his eyes closed. Probably lost in some music.

Demarco tapped on the iPad and didn't even seem to notice a phone rang at all.

Stormy and Charlie were the only two paying any attention.

"I should've thought of that." Charlie grimaced.

"Unusual situation, Cutter. Next time, Ricard will make sure you're better equipped for your assignment." He pulled out the still ringing phone and walked it to her. "Answer it, and then shut it off, would you? I know you probably have family and friends who are wondering what happened to you."

Charlie took the phone. It was her mother. The only person worrying, she was certain. "Hello, Mom."

The plane sped up and rumbled down the runway, the whine of the jet engines deafening.

Charlie stuck a finger in her free ear. "I can barely hear you."

"Where are you?" The worry in her mother's voice was unmistakable. "Your dad said you needed your research and then left for some meeting yesterday. I don't know where you kept your documents, honey."

"I'm at work." The plane lurched forward, and Charlie almost lost the hold on her phone. The take-off tilted her sideways. "Everything should be on my old laptop. The one in the closet downstairs." She calculated if her mother could handle the many updates the operating system would want to accomplish after having been turned off for almost two years.

"What, Charlie?"

"At work." She had to shout into the phone as the plane engines drowned out her voice.

Demarco looked up from the iPad and gave her a frown. Her loud words had interrupted his concentration. Well, too bad for him. Her research was important. She needed it to support the team.

"My thesis materials are in the folder labeled 'Voynich' on my desktop."

"Boy-nitch?" Her mother's voice filled with confusion. "I don't know if I can figure this out, I'd better wait for your father—"

"No, Mom. I need these files as soon as possible. You can do it. It's Voynich. Do you have a piece of paper?"

"Hold on."

The entire team had their eyes on her. Charlie's cheeks heated. She turned her head away, so she could at least block out the staring eyes. Who cared if she looked foolish? She needed her research to do her job on the team and decipher those strange markings.

"Mom? Are you there?" The silence on the other end of the line made Charlie wonder if they'd lost connection during the takeoff.

"All right. I'm back, honey."

"Okay, it's V-O-Y-N-I-C-H. In a folder with that name on the desktop of my computer. If you could zip it and send me everything in there."

"Voynich, I see, how silly of me." Her mother giggled. "What an odd name."

"Yes, Mother, very odd." Her humiliation was now complete. "So please send me those files as soon as you can. Today would be great."

"Today? Well, I've got my cleaning to do, and then your father has some going away luncheon that I have to attend. You know how they like the officers' wives to be at everything."

Charlie could picture the eye roll on the other end of the line. Her mother hated formal events. "I'll be back in my office soon, and I'd love to have those files waiting. I need them for my new assignment."

"Why didn't you say so? I'll make sure you have them in an hour. How's that?"

"Perfect. Thanks, Mom."

"No problem, honey. Hope you can come see us for dinner one of these nights. We're only a couple of hours away from you. Well, not during rush hour, but you know what I mean. We'd love to have you. It's been a long time since you've been home."

"I'm sure I'll find a time to come visit. Maybe after I settle in on base."

"Yes, that would do. You just let me know."

"You got it." Charlie hung up the phone and walked it over to her boss. "Here you go, Commander."

"Do you need to transfer any of your phone numbers while I have it out?"

Without even a moment's hesitation, Charlie said, "No, I'm fine. I've got them memorized."

Kellerman had his headphones around his neck and stared at her. "Memorized? All of your contacts?"

She gulped. "Yeah, don't you?"

"Um, nobody does," said Kellerman.

"They don't?"

Stormy chimed in, "No, we don't."

Charlie decided it was best to reel in her big mouth. "Well, I mean my parents' number, my brother. You know, those numbers."

Stormy squished her eyebrows together, and Kellerman narrowed his eyes.

Charlie forgot sometimes about her unique ability to remember bits and pieces of data. It's what made her so good at languages. At least, that's what she told herself. Her brother Chad also had the same memory skills as she, so she never questioned it much. Sure, a few friends in college thought of her as 'weird,' but she'd heard of others with photographic memories. She'd shrugged it off back then, sure that there were a lot of other people like her and her brother in the world.

Apparently, that was not the case.

For the rest of the flight, Charlie spent time programming contact information and email addresses into her throwaway phone.

Unlike the flight out, nobody interacted much on the return trip. Maybe Ricard's absence had more of an impact on the team than she had been expecting. Or possibly everyone was tired. Had it been only yesterday when she'd shown up at headquarters?

When they landed back at Andrews Air Force Base Orr stood up and addressed the team.

"Tomorrow we'll need to rip through this data ASAP. I want preliminary reports by 1500." The commander pointed at Kellerman. "I want material analysis. The pod. Is it similar to other samples from last summer? Where did it come from? Why does it dissolve so quickly in water?"

Kellerman had taken back the iPad from Demarco and tapped on it rapidly. "Yes, sir."

"Demarco."

"Sir."

"The preserved blood and other evidence from the woods. I want you to escort those items directly to Dr. Stern. I've already contacted her, and she's ready to receive everything we collected this afternoon. I want you to leave directly from here and meet up with her at the lab."

"Yes, sir."

"Stormy."

The thirty-something redhead took a breath. "Yes, Commander."

"Catalog each item in the database as per usual. And give Cutter's cell phone an ID in the system for tracking, strip it of the photos, and then dispose of it. Zip all the photos and upload them to the photos folder on the share drive."

"Dispose of it?" Charlie couldn't help herself. "But I thought I'd get it back...eventually."

Demarco gave her a steel gaze from across the fuselage. She'd spoken out of turn, and he didn't like it.

"Sorry, Petty Officer," Orr said. He crossed his arms and leaned against the doorframe that led to the cockpit. "Those photos are highly classified, and there's no way to completely erase them from your phone. It will have to be destroyed. It's protocol."

"Oh." Charlie thought about the loss of data, passwords, links. Her whole life existed on that phone. No wonder Demarco wanted her to take pictures with her cell phone. Why hadn't he come prepared? Shouldn't he have been ready with a camera, if he knew what they might encounter?

She shot a glance at Demarco. He locked eyes with her for a moment. The strange look in his gaze unnerved her, as if he could read her mind. She looked away and shuddered at the cold wave of uneasiness that ran through her.

"You will be reimbursed for the loss, of course. Stormy can help you with the paper work when we are back to the office." Orr looked once again to Stormy. "Chief usually handles the equipment, but—"

"Absolutely, sir. No problem, sir." Stormy wrote a note in a small notebook in her lap, then looked at Charlie and grinned.

"Now, for your assignment, Petty Officer Cutter," said the commander with a slow drawl.

"Yes, sir?" Although Charlie already thought she knew what her assignment would be, perhaps Orr had something else for her to help with. She very much wanted to fit in with the team and feel as if she were contributing. Maybe all the odd feelings she had about Demarco and even Kellerman would disappear once they realized her usefulness.

"Will you be ready for a preliminary report tomorrow afternoon with your findings?"

Charlie prayed her mother figured out how to send her files. "Yes, I can be ready with a preliminary by then." It had been awhile since she'd been buried in Voynich files, but the idea of possibly making a connection between that ancient text and the symbols found inside the pod heightened her senses.

"Stormy will show you how to access the photos once she's uploaded them to the share drive."

Charlie nodded and sneaked a glance at Lisa Storm. Her heart warmed at the idea she wouldn't have to interact with Demarco in order to do her job. In fact, maybe she'd hardly have to work with him at all. Even on such a small team, the division of work was definite. All of her time should be spent on language analysis, an area in which he had no expertise.

Her mind lit up at the notion of returning to her beloved research. It didn't matter to her that a connection to an alien pod and an ancient document made zero sense. Could she piece together the two examples and possibly decipher a meaning? An electric thrill zinged through her.

———

Wearing a crisp, fresh white uniform with her hair styled, Charlie made quick work of the security line the next morning. She slid her badge into the reader with confidence and sailed through to the hallway beyond. In her arms she carried a stack of papers—her research. She'd printed it out using the base motel's office printer, her temporary housing until she could find a permanent residence.

Excitement bubbled to the surface as she entered the elevator and rode down to the correct floor. She itched to reexamine the photos she'd taken in North Dakota.

The elevator door opened. People exited.

Demarco stood glowering in front of her.

"Petty Officer Cutter. Just the person I was looking for."

"Oh?" Instead of making a right turn and heading down the hall to her new office, Demarco grasped her elbow and maneuvered her back inside the empty elevator. "Excuse me?"

His warm hand on her bare, cool arm sent a shiver up her spine.

"I'm taking you to Dr. Stern's office with me."

The elevator door shut, and they were alone.

"Agent, I have work to do this morning." Charlie used his formal title to remind herself what a jerk Angel Demarco could be. "Commander Orr gave me an assignment and—"

Demarco released her arm and leaned against the brass rail that ran around three sides of the elevator. "You have plenty of time to put together a report before this afternoon's meeting. I want you to meet Dr. Stern. She's an important part of our team."

Charlie's hackles relaxed. It was a kind gesture. "I appreciate that. I suppose I could spare a few minutes."

"Plus," Demarco said with a wry grin, "she doesn't like me very much. Maybe you can break the ice with her."

"Someone doesn't like you?" Charlie asked. "Shocking." She raised an eyebrow.

"Don't tell anyone I said that." His typically controlled features relaxed into a genuine smile with a dimple.

When did he have a dimple?

As Charlie reexamined her feelings toward the special agent, he continued, "I've been insisting Dr. Stern and I are on good terms because I have the experience dealing with evidence. I have the training. I need to do the job. But if Orr found out there was friction between us, well, I can imagine Kellerman jumping right in to 'help.'"

"Your secret's safe with me."

"Thanks."

The elevator slowed as it reached their destination.

Charlie followed Demarco into a well-lit hallway on the fifth floor. Even though none of the floors had real windows—

any truly secure building couldn't have them—the designers of the facility had gone to a lot of trouble to ensure the lighting gave the appearance of natural light. The basement wasn't afforded such amenities.

"She's right down here."

At the end of the very long hallway they approached an unmarked door with a keypad on the outside and a card reader similar to their office down below. Access control in a top secret environment didn't stop at the front entrance.

Demarco slid his badge into the reader and entered a long string of numbers. He didn't share the code with her, which surprised her. But maybe this would be her one and only time visiting with Dr. Stern.

The door buzzed, and Demarco opened it.

———

They entered a most bizarre place.

Dr. Stern's office was smaller than anticipated. No larger than a two-car garage. It was jammed full of equipment and small fridges and chemicals and test tubes. But what caught her by surprise was the decor.

At first, Charlie could only marvel at the random canvases on the wall. Amateur art. Mountain landscapes, beach scenes, a chicken, a wine glass, poorly proportioned fruit. All painted in garishly bright colors.

"Who's this?" a honey-coated voice asked. "And where are my samples you promised last night?"

Charlie drew her gaze away from the paintings. A stout, middle-aged woman with sepia-toned skin, warm brown eyes, and hair cut close to the scalp peered at her over reading glasses as she sat at a utilitarian metal desk in one corner of the room.

Demarco cleared his throat, and his face reddened.

Charlie held back a laugh. Big, tough Angel Demarco scared of something. Delightful.

"This is Petty Officer Charlene Cutter. She joined our team two days ago."

"Well, aren't you a pretty little thing?" Dr. Stern said.

Charlie's cheeks heated at the blunt compliment. "Thank you."

"And polite, too." She cracked a broad white smile. "So glad to see more women in A Group. It was starting to smell like a locker room down there."

Demarco redistributed his weight from one foot to the other.

"And the samples?" Dr. Stern's tone turned decidedly colder. "You didn't screw it up again, did you?"

Charlie bit her tongue. This was too good.

"There was a delay in transport from Andrews. We expect everything to arrive here within the hour."

"I see. You think I don't see through this little thing going on here?" Dr. Stern waved a finger. "Trying to deflect from your incompetence by bringing this nice young lady with you?"

"No. Not at all."

Dr. Stern leaned back in her chair and crossed her arms. "Uh-huh."

"Cutter—" Demarco began.

Dr. Stern corrected him, "Petty Officer Cutter."

"Yes, Petty Office Cutter." Demarco stumbled over his words, "She, ah, well now, she's new—"

"You said that."

"And she's an important part of our team."

News to Charlie's ears. He'd made her feel as if she were

more of a nuisance and only good for handing off boring tasks he didn't want to do.

"Really? Well, then." Dr. Stern turned her gaze back on Charlie. "What is it they want you to do on the team?"

"I'm a linguistics expert. My specialty lies in deciphering ancient texts. Specifically the Voynich Manuscript. In fact—" Charlie opened up the manila folder filled with her graduate work and flipped through the stack of papers. "I managed to access my graduate work and was about to start in on some comparisons when Agent Demarco asked me to come with him."

Dr. Stern rose from her chair, a spark of interest in her eyes. "How fascinating." She plucked the top paper from the stack. "Although I have a knack for science, I always wished I had the gift to learn another language."

"Scholars haven't been able to decipher this one. It's been centuries." As she explained the mystery of the text on the page, Charlie's heart skipped a beat. That old excitement she'd had in graduate school, that she'd thought she'd lost, roared back to life with the merest hint of interest from Dr. Stern. "The script has no relation to any other written language on earth. At least no relationship that bore out a translation."

The scientist dropped the sheet on top of the stack of papers in the folder. "When you're done with your work, I'd love to learn more about it." She gave a quick smile and turned her gaze back on Demarco. "She'll be presenting her work to the team, I assume, at some point."

Charlie's confidence grew in that moment. From newest member of the team with zero clue, to expert on a topic that interested a scientific mind with years of experience. Maybe her work had meaning and usefulness after all.

Demarco swallowed. "Yes, I'm sure she will. We highly respect her expertise in the field."

Charlie almost fainted at the gushing praise. It must've taken all of the special agent's energy to make such wild claims. He didn't believe a word of it, she was certain. "I'm hopeful the photographs we took yesterday will help me build working knowledge of the writing. It did have a remarkable similarity." For a split second she thought about what that could mean for human history. Could an alien species have been present on earth centuries ago and gone undetected?

"I'll be on the lookout for the invitation then." Dr. Stern touched Charlie on the shoulder.

The door buzzed. Someone in the hall announced their presence.

CHAPTER 12

"THE SAMPLES." Demarco rushed to the door.

Dr. Stern snapped on the red siren light, which indicated possible uncleared personnel entering the room. Without the appropriate clearance, the only way someone outside could gain entrance would be for all cleared materials to be hidden from view or placed in a secure drawer or cabinet.

"Give me a moment." Dr. Stern quickly swept a stack of papers into a desk drawer. "Okay, we're good."

Angel Demarco opened the door. Two army privates in camouflage, one male and one female, rolled in a cart with a couple of the hard cases that had traveled with A Group on the plane.

"Your signature, ma'am." One of the privates handed Dr. Stern the transfer paperwork required.

"Thank you very much." Dr. Stern inked her signature with a grand flourish.

The two exited the room, and Dr. Stern snapped off the red siren light.

"The samples you wanted." Demarco unlocked the cases.

"Chief was attacked in the woods as he was carrying it to our bus, so there's substantial damage to some of the vials."

The case opened, and the smashed vials were revealed enclosed in plastic baggies to preserve as much as possible.

"There might be dirt in there, too, I had to pick everything up off the forest floor," said Charlie.

"You touched the materials with your bare hands?" Dr. Stern's brows shot up.

Demarco did nothing to rescue her from the question.

"Someone attacked the chief. I was in a bit of a hurry." Her explanation sounded weak to her own ears.

Dr. Stern looked over the contents of the first case. "This looks like mostly pod materials, similar to what was recovered last summer. But I'll do some tests to make sure it's the same unusual make-up."

Demarco unlocked the second case to reveal the extra pod samples Stormy had collected. "It disintegrated pretty rapidly after we arrived. But we managed to capture biological material." He pointed to a single shard of glass enclosed in a test tube on which a smear of red appeared. "Maybe Chief's attacker."

"Suspected alien DNA?" the doctor asked with a hint of awe in her voice.

The special agent hesitated and took a quick sideways glance at Charlie. He was holding back with her in the room. Charlie could sense it. He'd told her on the beach that he hadn't seen anyone in the woods when she'd found those odd footprints.

"I saw strange footprints in the sand near the crash site," Charlie plowed ahead. She didn't care if Demarco was pissed. "They didn't look human."

"Oh?" Dr. Stern carefully plucked the sample with the biological material from the case. She held it up to the fluorescent lights above her and examined it. "We were so close last year to obtaining a sample from another crash site, but then the vial disappeared along with a few others. That's when I instituted a policy about sample transport for the team, isn't that right, Agent Demarco?"

Charlie understood now why Dr. Stern had no love for Demarco. He'd screwed up somehow in the past.

"We have to go, doctor." He headed for the door. "We both have to work on our reports for this afternoon. Isn't that right Petty Officer?" He gave her a hard stare almost daring her to defy him.

"Yes." Charlie wanted to spend more time with the interesting doctor. She'd learned more about her team in ten minutes with Dr. Stern than in the last twenty-four hours.

"Please stop by again," said Dr. Stern who focused intently on the open cases in her laboratory rather than on the exiting visitors. "I'll have results for you in a day or two, if you could let Commander Orr know."

"Will do." Demarco slipped outside into the hall with Charlie not far behind.

The door shut with a kerthunk.

He headed down the hall toward the elevator without a word.

Charlie thought over the news about disappearing vials and wondered about the bus break-in at the motel in North Dakota. She'd need to keep her eyes and ears open. Perhaps her co-workers weren't as trustworthy as they let on.

———

Charlie sat at her newly assigned desk in the A Group office and pored over her Voynich research. Stormy had showed her how to navigate to their secure shared drive where the photos she'd taken yesterday were stored. As she scrolled through them, her fingers tingled. The symbols looked incredibly similar to the Voynich Manuscript.

The whorls and swirls of letters that edged the ancient text were repeated on pieces of the partially disintegrated pod. She had to set aside her disbelief at how this was possible and focus on the deciphering.

In her research, she had attempted to find repeated symbols that were the most common in order to break the code. Although the manuscript had been named after the Polish book dealer who purchased the manuscript in 1912, the assumption was the original author of the manuscript was Italian because of the vellum on which it had been written. So she had used Italian writing from the fifteenth century as a first comparison. Then she'd used basic decoding to attempt to figure out an alphabet of sorts. It was at that stage she'd hit a wall. Frustration and lack of confidence had resulted in her quitting the pursuit of her masters' degree and joining the Navy to do something else she loved: learning languages.

But with the new Voynich-like markings found within the pod, she had a possible association for each 'word' in the photo.

"Hungry?" Kellerman peered over her cubical wall.

Charlie's stomach rumbled. She'd been so focused on her work she didn't even realize how much time had passed. "When's our meeting this afternoon?"

Kellerman came around the cubical wall and took control of her mouse. He leaned in and navigated to her calendar. "Here."

He smelled of shaving cream—a not unpleasant smell—but Charlie rolled her chair back to put some distance between them.

"I'm sorry." He backed up aware he'd invaded her personal space. "It was easier to do it myself. Sometimes I can act without thinking." He pointed at the calendar that appeared on her screen.

Charlie, not wanting to dismiss an attempt at friendliness, replied, "That's okay. I appreciate it. I couldn't even figure out my email this morning." She scooted closer to the screen to read the calendar appointment. "That's right. Fifteen hundred."

"So lunch then?" the young lieutenant asked. "I know the best choices in the chow line. Trust me."

"Sure." Why not? She needed to get to know her team mates and what better way than over a free military lunch. "Should we ask the others?" She stood up and scanned the office.

"I don't think anyone else is still here."

"What time is it?"

"Thirteen hundred."

"What?" She checked her watch. "Wow, did I lose track of time."

"I can be a lot like that sometimes." He pushed up his glasses and smiled.

"Well, show me the way, please. My stomach would be most grateful." She grabbed her purse and cover.

"Absolutely."

As they were about to head toward the door, her desk phone rang. She hadn't given the number to anyone yet, so she stared at it for several seconds.

"Are you going to answer that?" Kellerman asked.

Confused, Charlie picked up the phone, "Petty Officer Cutter speaking."

"Good afternoon. It's Dr. Stern."

"Oh, Dr. Stern. I was wondering who might be calling." She glanced at Kellerman.

He sighed.

"Do you think you could stop by my office today?"

"Sure, is there something you need?"

"Your DNA."

The request made her forget about her hunger. "Excuse me?"

"You mentioned this morning you'd touched the samples, and I completely forgot to ask you for a DNA swab."

Charlie hesitated for a few seconds.

"It won't take more than a few minutes. You remember how to get to my lab, right?"

"Yes, I remember."

"Great. Right now would be perfect, if you don't mind. When I start on my testing plan, I don't like to be disturbed."

Kellerman gave her a questioning look.

"Sure, I could stop by in a few minutes. No problem." She shrugged, knowing her lunch date had no idea what she'd agreed to.

"Fabulous. Thank you, Petty Officer."

Charlie hung up.

"What did Dr. Stern want?" Kellerman asked. "I didn't even know you'd met her."

"We met this morning. Demarco took me to her lab."

The lieutenant pulled a grimace.

"I have to stop by to give her a DNA sample."

"Well, then let's go." He escorted Charlie to the door. "I'm starving, and I'd rather not eat alone."

They exited into the hall and headed to the elevator. "How long have you been with A Group again?"

"About nine months," Kellerman replied

"It's a relatively new organization. Do you still feel as if you are getting to know everyone?"

He pushed the 'up' button and then stepped back to wait for the elevator. "I suppose."

"How did you end up here?"

"Requested it." Kellerman kept his gaze on the closed elevator door.

Charlie mulled that over for a second. "How did you even know about it?"

"I have friends in high places maybe." He pushed the button again. "What about you?"

"Honestly, I don't know exactly. I was finishing up language school when I got orders to A Group."

"Must've been the commander. He seemed to know a lot about your background and your work."

The elevator dinged, and they climbed aboard.

"I guess." Charlie shrugged.

"What do you think about the assignment to our office?"

"I left my graduate program because I felt my research was going nowhere. But now I feel reinvigorated." Aware they couldn't discuss the details of their work outside their cleared spaces, Charlie kept the topic vague.

"Nice. That's sort of how I feel. I wanted to apply myself where I'd do the most good. My previous work—well, I was only a cog in the wheel. Not my thing."

"I get that." Although Charlie wanted to ask more about the work he'd done previous to the A Group assignment, she knew due to security reasons he wouldn't be able to share. She could only speculate what kind of work someone did at Area 51.

They reached Dr. Stern's lab and, since Charlie didn't know the code to enter, she pressed the call button on the wall to announce her arrival.

"Hopefully, it won't take too much time to give my sample," she said.

The door opened, and the red siren light flashed in her eyes.

"Lieutenant Kellerman, how nice to see you," said Dr. Stern. "You didn't take long acquainting yourself with Petty Officer Cutter." The doctor gave a knowing smile.

Kellerman's neck turned bright red.

"He was nice enough to ask me to lunch."

Dr. Stern eyed the tall man. "Is that so?"

"Yes, ma'am," answered Kellerman. He rubbed the back of his neck.

"Well, that's very kind. Come, let's take that sample so you can go to lunch then." Dr. Stern headed to a counter along the far wall. Several colorful paintings of farm animals stared down at them.

The doctor opened a drawer full of packaged swabs.

"I see you like to paint," Charlie said unable to keep her eyes off a painting of a black-and-white cow standing in a field of daisies.

The doctor unwrapped a swab and stood in front of Charlie. "Open wide please."

She opened her mouth. Dr. Stern swept the swab along her inner cheek on both sides.

"My cousin has one of those paint-and-sip places in Fairfax." She took the swab and popped it into its plastic container. "All done."

Charlie glanced around the lab. "You painted all of these?" There must have been two dozen paintings in all. Each one more colorful and ridiculous than the last.

"I find it an enjoyable way to pass the time." Dr. Stern walked them to the door. "If you by some chance have nothing to do one of these Saturday nights, I'm always looking for someone to come with me."

Charlie considered the idea. She and Dr. Stern with paint palettes and glasses of chardonnay making small talk while they painted together. She held back a laugh. Absurd. "I'll think about it. Thanks."

As they exited into the hall, Kellerman teased her, "Guess you made an impression on Dr. Stern."

Charlie lightly shoved him in the arm. "Oh, shut up."

His smile faded, and he grew quiet as they stepped inside the elevator.

———

Charlie and Kellerman arrived back at the office an hour before the All Hands meeting. Lunch had been awkward, but at least she'd filled her empty stomach with some halfway decent grub. Her lunch partner had helped her navigate the less trustworthy dishes and hone in on the better tasting ones. Free food had its shortcomings.

When they walked in the door, the deep voice of Chief Ricard greeted them, "I told 'em I wouldn't believe it unless I saw it with my own eyes—the LT on a date with the new girl." He grinned widely from his position by the coffee maker.

"Chief," Kellerman said, ignoring his teasing comment, "you look good."

Ricard touched a bandage above his ear. "A little knock on the head, nothing big. A few stitches, a couple of Motrin, and I'm back in tip top condition."

"That's good to hear." Charlie breezed past the implications of accepting a lunch invite from the young lieutenant. She'd have to make sure she didn't make lunch with Kellerman into a regular event. "I have a few things to wrap up before our meeting, if you don't mind."

Chief toasted her with his full mug of coffee. "By all means, Petty Officer. I don't want to keep a lady from her work."

She slipped past the two men who continued to chat about the chief's injuries. During lunch as she'd navigated the awkward conversation with the lieutenant, she'd found her mind half focused on the manuscript and the similarities in the writing in her photos. Kellerman sensed her disinterest at one point, as they'd eaten their cake slices in silence near the end of their lunch hour. She'd felt bad, but to rediscover an excitement about her research lifted her spirits more than she thought possible.

A couple of years ago, the whole project had hit a brick wall, and it had crushed her interest in continuing in the program. But with this new information, her mind came alive with all synapses firing. Furiously, she typed away at her preliminary report, taking snapshots of enlarged spots on her photos and inserting them next to similar images in the Voynich document. She added arrows and explanations, possible definitions, and a final conclusion that the two writings were definitely related.

Incredible.

With twenty minutes left before their meeting, she cobbled together a slide presentation for the office. The details were less complex and focused on a few examples she thought her team could understand without her background and education. Unmistakable similarities that could be explained no other way. She hoped Commander Orr would be impressed.

Her calendar appointment for the meeting popped up on her screen, breaking her concentration. She hit print, entered her code for tracking copies, and selected enough for everyone.

She scooped up the collated and stapled piles from the machine near the meeting room and handed them out to everyone seated at the big oval table and took an empty seat across from Stormy.

Commander Orr stood at the head of the table, a presentation laptop next to him, and a white screen on the wall. As he reviewed the print out she'd provided, Charlie's stomach flip flopped.

"Petty Officer Cutter," her boss said making eye contact. "Why don't you present first? Your report looks quite fascinating."

Charlie gulped.

She'd spent the whole day on her analysis. These people had no idea what she could add to the team. Even Charlie didn't realize, until she'd seen the writing in the pod, how perfectly suited she was for this assignment. The frustration she'd experienced when her orders had been unexpectedly swapped melted away as she approached the front of the room. Her discovery bubbled up inside like a mountain spring after a torrential downpour.

On the laptop, she navigated to the shared drive where she'd saved her slide presentation.

"Everyone, we might have made the discovery of a lifetime," Orr announced.

Stormy dimmed the lights.

The room was as quiet as a language exam during finals.

Charlie began to speak.

CHAPTER 13

"THE VOYNICH MANUSCRIPT is a document dating back to the fifteenth century." Charlie stood at the head of the table and scanned the meeting room. "The first owner known to history was Georgius Barschius from Prague in the seventeenth century. The document contained an unknown script and was intricately decorated with pictures of plants, stars, and chemistry annotations."

Charlie changed the slide, which displayed two snapshots of the manuscript side by side. The writing on the pages was strange and beautiful, full of odd loops and lines of text sprinkled throughout the colorful drawings, mostly of plants and flowers.

"Barschius sent a letter to Rome asking for help with the translation of the text. No one was able to translate the unusual writing."

She clicked to another slide that focused solely on the symbols that made up the mysterious language.

"Looks like elvish," Kellerman said. "You know, 'Lord of the Rings'?"

"Nerd." Demarco snickered.

Charlie ignored the two men and continued. "The next time the book appears it's 1912. An antiquarian book dealer named Wilfrid Voynich came into its possession, thus the name 'Voynich Manuscript' stuck. The sale was conducted in secrecy, but Voynich claimed he came across the manuscript in a chest in an ancient castle in southern Europe."

She clicked to the next slide—more pages of the manuscript, which depicted either the chronological year or other celestial events on circular drawings with intricate notes and pictures.

"Voynich became convinced that the cipher text must mean it was an important document. No other document from that time period had been written in code. Attempts were made to decipher it, but decades and centuries passed with no luck. Until now."

She clicked to the next slide. One of several photos she'd taken of the pod's interior before it had disintegrated in Devils Lake.

Stormy gasped.

"When I did a preliminary comparison of the writing inside the pod to the Voynich text, I found striking similarities between the two." She took her laser pointer and drew a circle of light around a symbol from the pod. "This one stood out to me immediately. It's repeated throughout the original text."

She clicked to a new slide showing a page from the Voynich Manuscript next to the pod photo.

"I'm sure you've all heard of the Rosetta Stone. It was the stone, which allowed for the translation of ancient Egyptian hieroglyphics into Greek. An incredibly important artifact that resulted in a whole new understanding of Egyptian history once the code was cracked. The writing from the pod that we were able to capture—this is our Rosetta Stone to decipher the Voynich Manscript."

She clicked to her last slide, which showed every distinct symbol she was able to capture from the photographs with possible translations.

"Because the pod clearly was used as a transport object of some kind, I attempted to understand the meaning of a symbol based on its relation to the interior of the pod." She used her laser pointer again to draw attention to a symbol next to what looked like a seat belt or restraining device made of the same gelatinous material as the pod. "This symbol probably has something to do with safety, latching, belting, locking." She pointed at another symbol next to a handle in front of the seat. "This symbol probably is related to movement: forward, backward, faster, slower."

The room was silent. She knew they were likely as excited by this discovery as she.

"I know it's a lot to take in. I'm only just beginning to examine these symbols and compare them to the ancient text. It took decades for the Rosetta Stone to yield results, so we can't expect instant translation. The next step will be to compare these early results to the text itself to see if I can find any like 'words.' That should help me untangle the meaning behind the manuscript."

She clicked to a final slide that said: "Questions?"

Commander Orr spoke first. "We don't have decades to translate this, Petty Officer. You are aware this a time sensitive project?"

His words of criticism hit like a physical blow. She'd thought they were silent due to amazement, but maybe she'd read the room incorrectly.

"I understand that, sir, but I am only one person."

"The one person specially brought on this team because we thought you had the expertise to translate this."

"I do have the expertise," she said.

"I am sensing that you are more interested in translating the manuscript rather than getting to the bottom of the writing inside the pod. This job isn't about pursuing your pet project on the government's dime."

"That's not what I thought, sir. Not at all."

"What I heard is that this will take decades of time. That it is impossible to produce a translation faster than that. What good does it do us to know that a symbol could maybe mean 'backward'? I need to know where these pods came from. Who was in them? What is their purpose? Why are they here? Your presentation, to be honest, was not up to the standard I was expecting at this meeting."

Charlie's face heated at the dressing down in front of everyone. "I'm sorry, sir."

"I have a question." Demarco tilted back his chair, drawing all eyes his way.

Commander Orr dropped his pen on his notepad and crossed his arms.

The special agent plowed forward, cutting through the tension in the air. "What do you think the connection is between this manuscript and the writing in the pod? What is your theory for the similarities?"

"Excellent question," she said. Who would've guessed Demarco would give her a lifeline? "If this team was assembled to study alien life on earth, then we must consider the possibility that a being traveled here in the ancient past using the same methods."

Stormy and Kellerman nodded their heads. The commander focused his gaze on his notes in front of him.

"Wouldn't that beg the question about the appearance of these supposed aliens?" Kellerman asked. "In order to blend in during the fourteen hundreds and create this manuscript, wouldn't the alien have to have the appearance of a human?"

"We don't know if an alien created this document," Demarco said.

"True," Charlie replied. "But the fact that no other document has ever been found with text similar to the Voynich manuscript would lead me to believe only a single being was capable of creating it. And perhaps something stopped this being from creating more than a single work."

"And for some reason these beings, as far as we know, didn't visit earth again until the last few decades," Kellerman added. "We need to figure out why."

"Agreed," said the commander. "I think Petty Officer Cutter has a lot of work ahead of her. It would be premature for us to speculate until she translates more of the text. I expect a more robust presentation next week." He gave her a pointed look.

Charlie exited out of her slides and returned to her seat.

"Special Agent Demarco, you're up next with your report about ambient conditions and their effect on the pod."

Demarco rose and took position at the head of the table.

Charlie wished she could sink into her chair and disappear. Although her fellow teammates had rescued her from further embarrassment with their questions, her stomach roiled at disappointing her new boss.

Demarco cleared his throat.

Charlie focused her attention on the front of the room.

The special agent winked at her.

She ducked her head and scribbled on her notebook, contemplating the nervous energy that filled her.

The office had grown eerily silent in the last hour. Charlie checked the time on her desktop computer: quarter past seven. The emptiness in her stomach reminded her she hadn't eaten in hours.

After the dressing down by Commander Orr in the meeting earlier, she'd buried herself in her translation work by comparing minute differences between symbols in the pictures and those in the ancient text. She would not disappoint her boss again. She could do the translation. She knew it. It would just take super human effort on her part to push past the first few 'like' symbols and wring out a definition that jibed with the pages of sample text she had.

The commander didn't understand translating the Voynich Manuscript using the symbols found in the pod was the key to understanding everything.

Her eyes burned from so much screen time in the darkened room. Charlie kept a small bottle of drops in her purse. She squeezed two in each eye, blinked a few times, and headed for the coffee at the back of the room.

She was startled to see Angel Demarco pouring the last of the coffee into a plain white mug. Hadn't he left with the rest of the gang a while ago? Ah, the door key. Only he and Orr had access to lock up the office for the night.

"Don't cry, Petty Officer." Demarco grinned and stirred powdered creamer in his mug. "We have some instant here somewhere." He opened up a lower cabinet to search.

She wiped her eyes. "It's eye drops."

"Gotcha." He winked for a second time that day and set the instant coffee jar on the counter.

Even though she wanted to say something biting, make fun

of him for winking at her or just irritate the hell out of him, she found she could not. He'd been too damned kind to her today. "Thanks for your question in our meeting."

"It was a good presentation." He stepped back to let her access the counter and craft herself a cup of instant. "Orr was out of line."

"I'm surprised you'd say that."

"He's the one that wrote up your orders and then he doesn't even give you the time to do your work? That's bullshit."

"Orr wrote my orders?" Although the commander had mentioned her graduate work on the plane to North Dakota, she hadn't really thought about how hands on he'd been with selecting her for the job.

"How else do you think you ended up here?" He gestured to the quiet, empty space surrounding them.

"I don't know—" Charlie couldn't think through the options. "He was familiar with the manuscript and my research, but I guess I thought orders came from BUPERS and went through a process."

"He'd gotten a scrap of writing last fall from another pod, ran it through a database, and that's when he found out about the manuscript. Who knew you'd also be a military linguist? He didn't have to convince you to come work for him, he could order you to do it."

"Another pod?" Although she'd been given the basic information about YARDARM, the last report in the folder had referred to a document that hadn't been provided to her.

"It wasn't in the packet?" He sighed. "After the arrival of the first one, when those two kids on watch duty at Fort Madison witnessed a pod landing in a storm, Orr started up A Group. He needed someone with a security background, and I volunteered." He stirred his coffee with a plastic stick. "There have been a few other incidents since then."

Her breath caught in her throat. More?

"Orr is obsessed with figuring this thing out. He's convinced the symbols are the key to understanding everything, and I think he's right. But he needs to give you time to do the work. Like you said, they didn't translate the Rosetta Stone overnight."

"I'm surprised you paid attention."

"Why would you say that?" He leaned a hip against the counter.

She pressed the special spigot on the sink and let hot water fill her mug. "You made it pretty clear yesterday that I'm a nuisance."

He studied her face. The intensity of his gaze unnerved her. "I don't think you're a nuisance. I think you could actually help me. I see that now."

Her stomach fluttered. She liked that he praised her work, but Stormy's words at the motel in Devils Lake floated in her mind: he had a sordid history with women.

"You hungry?"

"Starving," she answered without thinking.

"Let me take you out." Demarco downed his coffee in one swallow. "Don't want you to burn out. Since I'm your superior, I order you to stop working." He flashed a smile.

Sorry, Stormy, but she wanted to know what else Demarco knew. "All right. But it had better be good food." They'd be gone an hour or so, and then she could return to her work.

"I promise. It'll be the best Italian you've ever had."

As she followed him out of the office, the Voynich symbols floated around in her mind and organized themselves, much like her innate ability to learn new languages. A surge of dopamine washed over her. Although she'd explained to the team it would take time to translate, she'd held back the fact she knew far more than she was telling them.

"Italian sounds perfect."

———

Carmello's, Demarco's Italian restaurant of choice, was located a half-mile walk from their office at the Washington Navy Yard. The sticky August evening made Charlie aware that her anti-perspirant wasn't up to the challenge. Although she wore her Navy-issue black cardigan indoors to combat the air conditioned chill of the basement location, now the item stifled her.

"Can you hold this for me?" She handed her purse to the agent who wore a button-down shirt with tie and khaki slacks.

He held her purse like a football. "You don't have to wear your uniform to work."

She wrestled out of the sweater until she had stripped down to her summer whites—a short-sleeved cotton shirt and white cotton skirt paired with her sturdy black leather oxfords. "I'm still waiting on the movers."

"You didn't pack any casual clothes?"

She huffed, "They stuck me on a plane so fast I barely had time to grab my toothbrush."

He nodded, handed back her purse, and they continued on their way.

"So you're good at this translation stuff?" he asked.

She knew a free meal would come with an interrogation. Why else would he be interested in spending an awkward hour across the table from her? "I've always been good at words, languages, grammar." She shrugged. "One of my special gifts."

"Grammar, ugh."

She smiled. "What do they say? Learn a skill nobody else likes."

"That's true."

"I'm sure you have a few skills that come in handy from time to time." She thought back to that moment in the woods when an attacker had taken down two of their team.

"We all have our talents." He pretended to karate chop her shoulder. "Hi-yah."

Charlie let out a laugh at the goofball move. Not the same hardcore Demarco she'd met the first day. A warmth filled her chest, and she viewed the special agent in a bit of a new light for a fleeting moment.

A well-dressed couple strolling in the opposite direction gave them a wide berth. The female half of the duo scanned Charlie up and down before returning to her conversation with her companion.

Demarco sobered. "I know we can't talk details out here, but I'd like to understand as much as you can tell me."

"I gave you everything I had this afternoon. You think I'd hold out on the commander?"

"You've been at your desk for the last two hours. Seems as though Orr lit a fire under your ass."

He had, but Charlie didn't yet trust the special agent to share more.

As they reached the corner, someone bumped Charlie from behind and snatched her purse.

"Hey!"

The thief elbowed her in the side so hard, she stumbled and fell into the gutter.

"Are you okay?" Demarco reached out a hand.

"I'm fine." Dirty water from the gutter had splashed onto her pristine white uniform, making a mess. "He took my purse...and my security badge." A lump formed in her throat.

Demarco took off after the figure who wore sagging jeans and a white T-shirt. As her co-worker ran down the street chasing her assailant, he let out a string of obscenities.

The sting of scraped palms brought her back to her position in the gutter. Gross. Gracelessly, she stood and swiped her stinging hands on the back of her skirt, as if that would clean off the dirty water and trash she'd landed in.

Demarco disappeared around the corner.

Within seconds, the sound of shouting and tires squealing echoed down the block.

Charlie trotted toward the noise.

Her dinner date rounded the corner with her security badge in hand, a bloodied lip, and a wide smile on his stupidly handsome face.

CHAPTER 14

"THANKS," Charlie said putting on the badge, which she had affixed to a lanyard, and tucking it into her blouse for safe keeping. "That's the second cell phone I've lost in two days."

"Sorry I couldn't recover the whole purse for you, but that guy had an accomplice waiting." He brushed his hands on the legs of his khaki pants.

"I heard." She sighed. Her best summer whites were ruined. "Looks like I'll be buying new uniform items at the Px tomorrow. This was my best skirt."

"My place is a few blocks from here." He stood with hands in his pockets. "You can borrow some of my clothes. We can order a pizza."

From casual dinner in a public place to private pizza party for two at his apartment? She bit her lip.

"I feel as if I need to make it up to you. I'm the one that wanted to go to Carmello's." Already he was tucking in his button-up shirt that had pulled loose from his khakis and straightening his basic, boring red tie.

One-hundred percent anal.

And what would such a person's apartment look like? She had to admit a gnawing curiosity made her say, "All right. Pizza it is."

He wiped his brow with his arm. A sheen of sweat glistened for a moment and then disappeared. Angel transitioned from thief-chasing hero to unsmiling agent in seconds. "Follow me."

They headed across the street from the corner and passed by rows of federal-style townhouses adorned with black wrought iron railings and matching black shutters, which set off the attractive brick-red exteriors. Mature red maple and sweet gum trees lined the edges of the sidewalks and, since it was the bloom of summer, provided a pleasant canopy. Between the matching townhomes stood less elaborate, boxy two story homes painted cream or blue, which gave a patriotic flair to the neighborhood.

"Have you lived here long?" Charlie imagined finding her own place to live. She'd requested off-base housing. "Seems like a perfect spot. You could walk to work."

"Eh, not long."

"Where were you before A Group?"

"I've spent my whole career in the DC area."

He didn't elaborate. Closed door. Do not ask again. The end.

"Here we are." He stopped in front of one of the many townhomes and headed for the stairs that led down into a basement section of the building. "I'm in the lower-level."

When she passed through the front door, she was transported to the jungles of the Amazon. Where a living room and kitchen should be, potted plants of all sizes were the guests of honor. Trees, flowering plants, even vines, which crisscrossed overhead and spanned archways, filled the space to overflowing.

"Wow."

Demarco sat in a brown armchair that blended in with two seven-foot tall ficus trees and removed his shoes. "I like houseplants."

"I guessed as much." She stood in the entryway. "Should I —?" She lifted her foot and rested it on her thigh so she could remove one of her dress shoes.

"You don't have to."

Too late. She held the shoe in her hand and laughed.

His lips curled up as if he were bemused.

"After wearing these all day, it feels good to walk around barefoot." She removed her other shoe and pushed them to one side. To take it all in, she strolled around the apartment space. "You said you haven't lived here very long, but how did you manage to grow all of this so quickly?" She touched the thin, delicate stem of a bright yellow orchid flower and marveled at its beauty.

"I guess I have a green thumb." He punched a number on his flip-style phone and put it to his ear. "Pepperoni okay?"

She nodded. The lush surroundings made her forget about the theft on the street, the strangeness of her job, and the on-again off-again cold shoulder Demarco displayed. Ferns, cacti, vines, trees, houseplants of every size and variety dazzled the eye.

She reached the kitchen. Fewer plants in this space, which made sense. How else would he be able to prepare food or eat when choked by greenery?

In the fridge she found a collection of locally-brewed beer. Why not? "Is it okay—?" She held up a bottle.

"Yeah, sure, bring me one. The pizza will be here in about thirty minutes."

"Sounds good." Charlie had intended to use their dinner out as a time to mine more information about their work. What she knew only scratched the surface, and today in the meeting, the urgency Commander Orr had displayed made her think there was more going on at a higher level. The more intimate setting had relaxed her and threw off her focus.

She handed him the beer.

"Oh, the clothes I promised." Demarco set his beer on a glass side table dotted with African violets and trotted through the kitchen into a short hallway beyond.

Left alone, she grew more curious about how the special agent lived. She hunted for books, DVDs, magazines, anything that might give her a window into the man inside. Oddly, she couldn't find a thing. Shelves hidden by hanging vines only revealed potting soils and fertilizers. In fact, she couldn't even find a television. Where one should be, across from the sofa on a wide expanse of wall, he'd hung shelves on which to set more plants.

Maybe he'd given over this space to his plants and those normal living room items were kept in the bedroom?

"Will this work?"

She had her head inside one of his kitchen cupboards and jumped at his voice. "I'm starving. Hope the pizza is delivered soon." She grabbed a couple of plates to cover her snooping.

Demarco held a gray T-shirt and a pair of running shorts with an adjustable waist. "You're tall." He tossed them at her.

"Thanks. Where can I change?"

"There's a guest bath right there." He pointed out a door hidden by more plants. "Then maybe you want to use my phone to cancel your bank card or something?"

"Dammit." Not only that, but her military ID. What a pain in the ass that was going to be.

"Give me a minute to change." Charlie locked the door and quickly slipped out of her ruined uniform. She caught sight of herself in the oval mirror above the sink. Dirt smudged her cheek and strands of hair had slipped loose from her French braid. She turned on the water and scrubbed her face clean in her underwear before donning Demarco's clothes.

The T-shirt smelled like him. Clean, yes, but a subtle masculine fragrance she couldn't place. Then she attempted to tuck the loose strands of hair back into formation. When the improvement to her appearance was minimal, she sighed, folded up her uniform and joined her dinner companion.

"It fits okay." She stood in the dining space with her arms out to her sides and spun around. "Do you have a bag I could put my stuff in?"

Demarco leaned against the kitchen counter, arms crossed, and regarded her for a moment. He opened a drawer next to him and grabbed a plastic grocery bag. "Here you go."

As she slipped her uniform into it, a question popped out of her mouth, "You never did tell anyone what happened in the woods."

"We're not in the office, Cutter."

"It's a simple question, not attached to any particular incident or location. What did you see in the woods?"

His gaze burned into hers. "I didn't see anything."

"Bullshit."

The doorbell rang, which was followed by a loud knock.

"Pizza's here." He handed Charlie his flip phone. "Why don't you make that phone call?

She gripped the phone tightly. "What did you see, Angel?"

He visibly stiffened.

Demarco carried the pizza box to the small table in the dining area, dodging the extended branches and leaves of his plant collection.

Charlie stood with phone in hand.

"Make the call." Whipping open the pizza box, he grabbed a large slice, folded it in half and took a bite.

"I don't have the number."

He set his half-eaten slice on the open lid of the pizza box and retrieved his bottle of beer from the other room. "You seem to have every other phone number memorized."

"Family, friends, yes. Random bank emergency numbers, no." She grabbed a plate and chose a slice of pizza. "Why won't you talk about the person you chased in the woods? Doesn't that have to be part of your report?"

He sat at the table and finished off his first slice. "Have I done my job as the security expert on the team? Yes. Do you need to know everything? No."

As she ate, she mulled over his answer.

"Would you sit down, please?" He kicked out the empty chair. "You're making me nervous hovering there."

She took him up on the offer. "By your answer, I will make my own assumptions, then."

"Fine." He picked up a second slice and drank a swig of beer.

"The only way I can fully support the team is by completely understanding what we are up against. I feel as if I only have a little peek inside rather than an invite to the party. Why? Doesn't everyone want me to connect the dots?"

"You've been here for two days. Maybe slow it down. Focus on your work."

Charlie had hit a wall. "Do you have any family? Brothers? Sisters?"

"Why do you want to know?" Resting both fists on the table, he paused his eating.

"I was making casual conversation. Is that not allowed?"

He rubbed his chin. "I had family once." A slack expression appeared.

When he didn't elaborate, Charlie abandoned the desire to press for more. Maybe Stormy knew more about Demarco's past.

"Tell me about your family." His gaze softened, and he leaned back. "I know you have a mother and a father."

Her face heated. He'd overheard more than one private conversation when she wasn't on her best behavior. "And a brother, Chad."

"Chad and Charlie." He smirked. "Cute."

She sighed. After joining the military, answering personal questions became rote. Every assignment, every new roommate, it was the same old thing.

"And where are Chad and Charlie from?"

If she opened up, maybe so would he. "We're Navy brats, which means we're from everywhere and nowhere." Maybe that would be enough of an answer for him.

"So you've traveled a lot."

"I guess you could call it that."

"I always wished I could travel more."

"Why don't you then?" she asked.

He hesitated and nodded his head. "You'd think it would be that easy, but sometimes things stand in the way of what you want."

His words resonated with her in a way he probably didn't expect. She kept her thoughts to herself. "Look, it was nice of you to offer dinner and all of that, but we don't need to be friends, you know."

"I know." He scanned her face.

The scrutiny unnerved her.

"What do you want from me?" Her stomach turned sour, and her appetite fled.

"Why do you think I want something from you?"

Dressed in his clothes and sitting in his kitchen, she felt vulnerable. The desire grew to leave his strangely decorated apartment. This was too intimate a setting for two co-workers who'd only just met. Stormy's words rang in her head about Demarco's reputation. "I should really go back to base and call my bank." She pushed her plate away.

"Let me give you a ride. I'm parked right out front."

"That's not necessary." She carried her plate to the sink and grabbed her clothes. "I know my way back."

"I insist."

She worked hard to keep her expression neutral.

"Ah," he said, casually closing the pizza box and gathering their empty beer bottles, "you don't trust me. What do you think I'm going to do?"

Her body froze, and her heart thudded. "I don't want you to go out of your way for me."

"It's really not a problem." As he set his plate in the sink, his arm brushed hers. "You just had your purse stolen. I don't think Commander Orr would be too appreciative if his linguistics expert didn't make it in to work tomorrow."

"I'm going to walk." She backed away from him. "Follow me, if that's what you want." The scent of the borrowed shirt hit her nose, and the once beautiful indoor jungle pressed in on her.

———

Charlie walked at a brisk pace, Demarco a few steps behind. Why didn't he turn around and go home? The best way to purge her growing discomfort was to change into her own clothes, maybe swim a few laps. Yes, a good swim would straighten her out in no time. It always did.

But having the special agent hot on her heels didn't help. He was half the reason she wanted to be alone...the other half? Well, the other half continued to process the Voynich comparison. Although Orr had reprimanded her for giving the appearance of being more interested in translating the manuscript than figuring out the origin and purpose of the pods, he didn't know what she'd found buried in the manuscript. A possibility so bizarre and so mind boggling, she wanted to examine the manuscript further to be sure she was on the right track.

"You missed the turn," Demarco corrected gently. "Tingey Street."

Without saying a word, she made a left turn onto the next block.

"That will loop you back to Tingey."

"Excellent," she snapped.

By the time she reached the base motel, her temporary home, most of her anxious energy had worn off. Her walking companion had kept his distance, and she grew used to his calm directions if she veered off course.

When she reached the doors of the motel lobby, she paused and faced him, "Thank you, but as you can see I made it back safely."

Demarco stood ten feet distant and absently played with the wristband of his watch. "I hope you have a good evening, Charlie."

She nodded and entered the lobby. Instead of continuing to her room on the second floor, she found a window that looked out toward the parking lot. Demarco stood at the edge of the curb, waited for a car to pass, and then headed back in the same direction they had come. She lingered there, unable to leave until his figure became a distant blur.

Ten minutes later she exited her motel room in a fresh white uniform—white blouse, with name tag and medals transferred from the stained one in the plastic bag, and white pants pressed perfectly with creases down the middle. Although she longed for a swim to soothe her nerves, her mind focused on her obsession: the manuscript. It waited for her back in her office. A desire to dig deeper, work harder, and confirm what she believed gnawed at her.

The base had grown quieter. The summer sun had set, and twilight lit up the deep blue sky with an eerie glow.

She crossed the base and entered the main building. A few offices ran 24/7 operations, so it was not unusual for someone to run their badge this late in the evening. A single guard sat on a stool near the card readers. As she ran her card through the access control slot, he barely looked up from the magazine he read

The green light appeared. She pushed through the turnstile. Once she reached the elevator, she realized her mistake: the key. She couldn't enter the office now that someone had returned the key, and that someone had been Demarco when they'd left together to eat dinner.

Dammit.

Yes, she knew the code to enter the office, but she'd forgotten about the key system Stormy had pointed out on her first day.

She abruptly turned and exited through the turnstiles.

This time, the guard watched her carefully as she left. Her unusual entrance and exit caught his attention. She was sure someone would ask about that at some point. Would it travel back to the office? To Commander Orr? To Demarco?

Her stomach soured at the thought Demarco would know. He'd left her at the motel, and she'd given the impression she was headed to her room.

She let out a breath and pushed through the front door and into the summer evening.

———

The gym stood open twenty-four hours a day. The advantage of being on a military schedule and having to maintain fitness was that access to workout spaces was unlimited. She slipped inside the quiet building, nodded to the solitary individual tasked with working the desk overnight, and entered the women's locker room.

Empty.

She disrobed and donned her one-piece suit, a plain navy blue one she'd received at Boot Camp. Not the most flattering, but it had been free. The constant chlorine exposure had started to wear down the elasticity, and she knew before too long, she'd have to purchase another. Maybe tomorrow after work when she visited the Px to pick up new uniform items, she could find a replacement suit.

She stowed her dry clothing, gym bag, and shoes in a locker, and then stood in front of a full-length mirror to brush out her braids and pull her hair into a ponytail. Sculpted biceps and shoulders stood out to her, a different body than she'd had before going to Boot Camp. She'd always been moderately interested in exercise, but in Boot Camp she'd found a natural gift for sport. She'd never pushed herself. But her RDC made sure she was motivated to strive beyond her normal physical limits.

A love of swimming kept her coming back to the pool. Although all Navy personnel were required to take a physical fitness test twice yearly, she had the choice of a one-and-a-half mile run or a five-hundred-meter swim.

But the physical changes to her upper body surprised her. She flexed her arm to see the result and hoped that regular swimming would maintain that new shape.

Although the sign next to the door to the pool read 'closed,' she'd bypassed signs before in Monterey. The lack of a lifeguard didn't bother her, and nobody was going to be checking this late in the evening to make sure the pool was clear. Most sailors preferred using the treadmills and ellipticals than the pool.

The lights were turned off, but enough residual light flooded through the windows on the double door entrance from the hall that she'd be able to make out the numbers on the lap clock. She wanted to improve her times before her fitness test in October.

She chose the lane closest to the locker room door in case she ran into a problem. But seeing as how the person sitting at the entrance barely acknowledged her, well, she wasn't worried. She slipped on her goggles.

Making a sleek dive, she knifed into the eighty-five degree water. The first few laps she warmed up with a relaxed breast stroke.

One. Two. Three. Four.

Perfect rhythm. She hung onto the edge for a few seconds,

pushed off, and switched to freestyle. Each breath, each stroke was as natural as walking.

Her work on the manuscript occupied her thoughts. The odd shapes and swirls looped in her mind, soaring in and out, placing themselves in patterns on a black canvas. Creating words and meaning out of gibberish. She closed her eyes. Barely aware of her body.

Instructions. But for what?

A recipe for an organic compound. Weight and measurements. Types of plants.

A page floated ahead in the dark. A wheel of symbols and letters. It rotated faster and faster and faster. A blur. An impossible blur. Time passing. Hours? Days? Years?

Her fingertips slammed into the concrete.

She gasped and grabbed the solid edge.

An electric zip ran through her.

A machine.

The writer of the manuscript had been building an organic machine.

"Cutter, you swim?" Commander Orr stood in the shadows of the closed pool room, a white towel looped across his neck. He whistled. "Did you compete? That was an amazing lap time."

Charlie whipped off her goggles. "Sir?" An answer escaped her. An organic machine rotated in her mind, made of plant material. Layer upon layer, built by hand. Crafted by a long-dead mystery creature. Orr's questions rankled her. She pushed herself out of the pool. Water ran off her body.

"Didn't mean to interrupt your workout. Thought I was the only one who swam off hours."

She padded to her towel. "That's okay." She wrapped it tightly around her. "I need to go."

"Petty Officer, you don't need to."

"See you tomorrow, sir. Oh-seven-hundred." She squeezed water out of her ponytail. "I've got a lot of work to do. So much work." Her heart sped up.

The creature in the ancient past had been building a pod.

CHAPTER 15

"HERE YOU GO." Chief Ricard handed Charlie a brand new iPhone in the office the next morning. "To replace the one we had to take."

"Did Demarco—?" She scanned the small office for the agent's dark head. Across the room, she spied him through the window of Orr's office deep in conversation.

Ricard powered it up. "I programmed it with all your numbers and contacts." To prove it to her, he scrolled through her contacts list. "Can you sign this?" He handed her a receipt form and a standard black government ballpoint pen that looked to date back to the 1980s.

"Uh, sure." She scribbled her name and handed it back. Later on today, she needed to find a free moment to call her bank and report her stolen card amongst other things.

"Great." As he was about to walk away, he changed course and snapped his fingers. "Almost forgot. Orr wants to see you in his office." He pointed at the now open office door.

Demarco had disappeared.

"Thanks." She set her new phone on her desk and took a few sips of hot coffee to steel herself for the meeting. Although

Orr had been kind last night at the pool., she didn't want a repeat of the All Hands meeting yesterday.

She grabbed a pen and a yellow legal pad and knocked on the open door. "You wanted to see me, sir?"

He waved her in. "Come on in, Petty Officer. Have a seat." He gestured at two empty chairs in front of his desk. "And close the door."

She clasped the legal pad closely to her chest and pressed her knees together. Her jaw clenched down. Stress filled every pore.

Orr tented his fingers and leveled his gaze. "I wanted to apologize to you."

Lightness filled her.

"My reaction yesterday in our meeting was unprofessional. I should've expressed my thoughts in private with you and not in front of the whole group."

She stared back. A million responses formed: *Thanks. No problem. It's okay. I'm over it.*

A drink of water would really help.

The phone on his desk rang.

"Give me a second here." He answered, Orr speaking."

Charlie's armpits were damp. Although she'd gotten past the fear of further reprimand, why hadn't her body received the notice?

"You're sure?" Orr broke out in a smile. "Hot damn, that's fantastic." He focused his gaze on Charlie and widened his eyes. He nodded. "Excellent. Thanks for your work on this."

He hung up.

"Looks like we got a radar signature."

"A what?"

His demeanor had made a one-eighty shift from serious apology to exuberant joy.

"A signature. A goddamn signature." He opened the door and stepped into the office. "We can track the pods, everyone. Holy hell, we can track the pods." He let out a whoop and smacked his hands together.

Charlie clutched her precious yellow pad. Was their meeting over? Should she leave?

Ricard and Stormy hugged.

Kellerman did a fist pump.

Demarco stood aloof and off to one side, as if a dark cloud had settled directly over him. No expression. No reaction of any kind. The usual Demarco moodiness.

"I've told them to keep us all apprised. If that radar signature shows up again, anywhere in the world, you'll all know about it immediately. This means everyone is on call. You receive a text about it, we all meet back here ASAP no matter the day or time. Prepped and ready to go. Got it?"

"Yes, sir," Ricard saluted.

"Got it, commander," Charlie said. Even more pressure to have a go-bag ready. Screw the moving truck, she'd have to give in and buy some civvies that very afternoon.

"And that means for the next ninety days, at least, no leave is approved."

Stormy frowned.

"We seem to be in some kind of pattern here. Three pods in a years' time. We can't risk missing the next one. We need an intact pod to move our research further along."

Charlie hovered behind Orr. "Sir, if you don't mind?"

"Sorry." He stepped to one side to unblock the door. "Second apology of the day. That's a rare thing, Petty Officer." He laughed a booming laugh. "Enjoy it while you can."

"Yes, sir."

. . .

Kellerman stood near her cubicle. "That's some very awesome news."

"Yeah."

"You sure lucked out being assigned here when you did. The last six months have been boring as hell."

"What did he mean by three pods?" She didn't intimate that Demarco had shared with her the additional pod arrival.

He ticked off with long, lean fingers. "Last July at Fort Madison, December in Idaho near the Acoustic Research Center in Bayview, and then the latest one in North Dakota. The first two were before my time."

She fought to keep her expression neutral. "Any idea what they found at the sites of the other two? More Voynich remnants?" The images that entered her mind last night at the pool returned. More samples meant more confirmation that her translation was correct.

"The December pod was a bust. Landed on the shore rather than in the lake during a heavy snow and exploded into a million pieces from what Stormy told me. Any chance at recovery was blown. Any contact with water, and the pods and all their contents disintegrate. Pieces that small?" He blew air out his nose. "Not a chance."

The visual of a pod and all its 'contents' exploding made her nauseous. "Why so much time between landings?"

"How do we know we've gotten wind of all the pods?"

Charlie turned the information over in her mind. Her discovery couldn't be held back for long. She wanted to share with Kellerman what she'd found in the manuscript, but gut instinct held her back. "That's true. There could've been more. Earth is a large place."

"Well, the fact we now have a radar signature to track will

help with that. If pods are landing elsewhere, we will be the first to know about it."

"Do you really think aliens are in these pods, Lieutenant?" She leaned against the wall of her cubicle.

"What else could be the reason for them? The shape. The space inside. Even your preliminary translations point to a transportation device, levers and other functional items inside for a traveler."

"I know. But I still can't wrap my mind around it."

He rested an arm on the top of the cubicle and leaned in. "You'd be surprised at what we know." The young lieutenant's gaze darted down the aisle. "I can't really say much, but just accept it."

A tightening in her chest reduced her breaths to shallow ones. "You mean your work at Area 51?" she whispered.

Kellerman peered over the edge of the cubical walls and then focused his gaze on her. "Yes." He lifted an index finger to his lips and then shifted his weight. "I've been wanting to ask you something."

"Oh?"

He rubbed the back of his suddenly red neck. "I thought maybe you might want to go to a movie sometime or dinner?"

Her face heated. "Um." Not a single word entered her mind. Not one. If only a bolt of lightning would zap the building and knock out the power. That would be a welcome relief from the awkward pause. "Well, I—" *Do it. Give him a chance. Why not, Charlie?* What was she so afraid of? He was a nice guy.

Where did that coffee cup go? Her mouth dried up like the Sahara Desert.

The main door to the office swung open, and a recognizable voice filled the air.

"How are my team today?" Dr. Stern bellowed. "Where is everyone?"

The cubicle set-up hid a lot of the activity behind bland beige walls, but also kept the wrong eyes from accidentally glimpsing top secret work.

"Dr. Stern," greeted Commander Orr, his lips still locked in a joyful grin. "Please do come in. We'd love to have more good news today, wouldn't we, team?" He lifted his hands and nodded with eyebrows raised.

Kellerman sniffed and gave Charlie a glassy stare.

"Let's talk later," she whispered.

His shoulders slumped, and he faced Orr and Dr. Stern as they shook hands outside his office.

"Commander, nice to see you again. I know I don't normally show up in your office unannounced, but—"

"Not a problem. Not a problem. You're welcome anytime. You're one of the most important members on our team." He invited the doctor into his office. "We can talk privately, If you'd like."

With all of the morning's interruptions, how would Charlie ever finish the translation work? The commander expected pod translations, which she could probably figure out now, if she only had a quiet moment to spare.

"This concerns the whole team," said Dr. Stern. She had shed her lab coat and arrived wearing a very stylish mid-length dress in a lovely coral color and a pair of strappy heels. Out of her lab, the doctor came across as much younger than Charlie had originally surmised. "Can I use your meeting room?"

"Of course." Orr's face clouded. "Let's go team. We've got work to do, so let's make this quick."

Upset he didn't get first crack at Stern's news?

The team filled the chairs around the table and waited

expectantly for the doctor to share her findings. Charlie hoped for more about the possible occupant of the pod. The blood she'd managed to salvage could be connected to alien life.

Stern stood front and center, hands on wide hips. "I wish I had better news for you, but I wanted to deliver this in person to answer any questions you might have."

Demarco cracked his knuckles as he stood near the door. He'd chosen not to sit.

"The pod material collected was too contaminated for a complete analysis. I know this is disappointing. These were fresher samples, and we were all hopeful. The smashed vials had direct contamination from the forest, and the complete samples from Stormy had fully disintegrated in the water inside the tubes and bonded with the pod material similar to our last samples." She paced in front of the retracted projection screen. "The blood sample recovered by Petty Officer Cutter was a very small sample. The lack of material present required a different process for DNA analysis. Unfortunately, I cannot do that type of analysis at my lab here. I arranged for a lab at the National Security Agency to do the testing. It could take up to fourteen days for the results."

Orr pulled his chin. "This lab, do they have the appropriate clearance levels?"

"I made sure to discuss the sensitivity of A Group's work with the head of the lab, and he understood our concerns. They do highly sensitive work at that facility, and that is the reason I chose them. Your sample should be as safe there as it is in my lab." Dr. Stern scanned all the faces in the room. "Any other questions?"

Kellerman raised a hand.

Dr. Stern pointed.

"Will the results be available on the intranet here in the office, or will it be a printed report delivered?"

Strange question. What did it matter?

"A Group has a limited intranet here at Washington Navy Yard, but I'll attempt to have them deliver the report via secure networks. The printed report should be delivered with other top secret materials somewhere around that two-week time-frame. When it arrives, I will contact the team and give a presentation of the findings."

Kellerman rested his elbows on the table. "Sounds good."

"Anyone else?" Dr. Stern asked.

Stormy raised a hand. "Will I be able to make a copy of the report to keep in our files here in the office?"

"Yes. If the secure network avenue fails for delivery, I will make it available to you. I understand how important it is to keep track of each piece of evidence."

A classified copier sat in the main office space. They each had a personal code they had to enter to monitor what they printed on the machine. All copies were counted and tracked to ensure no one made inappropriate copies or walked out of the secure facility with documents they shouldn't have.

"Any other questions?" Dr. Stern waited a heartbeat or two. "I know this was not the news you wanted to hear today. Time is passing quickly to decipher the origin and meaning of the pods, but I want you to know I'm in this with you for the long haul. I won't let you down. We will hopefully find something meaningful in the blood evidence that may further our under-standing of what's happening. I'm still excited I was chosen to be part of this amazing team, so don't lose focus on the bigger picture. We can piece this puzzle together and find out why these pods are here. I'm sure of it."

"Thank you, Dr. Stern," said Commander Orr. "We very

much appreciate the time you took out of your busy day to deliver this news personally."

"My pleasure." Dr. Stern smiled. "This is the assignment of a lifetime."

"Well, everyone, looks like it's back to work. Demarco, I want that write-up on Devils Lake by the end of the day. Kellerman and Ricard—meeting at 1100 to go over the details of the attack." All three men nodded. "Doctor, before you go, I'd like to meet with you in my office for a moment, if you could."

"Of course, Commander. But could you give me a minute?" She made eye contact with Charlie and smiled. "I have a question to ask your newest member."

Orr raised an eyebrow, but didn't ask any questions. "Petty Officer Cutter?"

"I'm happy to answer whatever questions you might have, doctor." Charlie smiled.

The commander ushered everyone out of the conference room and left Dr. Stern and Charlie alone.

"You wanted to ask me something?" Charlie remained seated and viewed the older woman who had a spark to her brown eyes.

"I do." Dr. Stern gave a quick smile and then sat in the chair right next to her. "I like you, Petty Officer Cutter."

"Well, that's kind of you to say." Her bewilderment at the statement was tempered by a warm feeling from the compliment. "Is there something I can help you with? Perhaps you wanted me to give you that overview of my findings so far?" Could she trust Dr. Stern with her discovery in the Voynich manuscript? She'd appeared very interested in her linguistics work upon their first meeting.

"I am definitely interested in your translation work, but my question is more of a social one."

"Oh?"

"I mentioned that my cousin runs a paint-and-sip business in Fairfax."

"Yes, I remember." How could she forget? The woman's whole lab was covered in proof of that statement.

"I'd like to invite you to a paint-and-sip class this Saturday at her studio." The serious scientist turned into a fun-loving artist within seconds. "She has a few spots left in her Starry Night Owl class, and I told her I could help her fill them. I'll pay for the whole thing, even buy you a glass of wine. She's been working so hard at this business, and I want to help her as much as I can. You're new to town. I thought maybe you'd be free and looking for something to do besides sitting on base."

"A painting class?" Charlie gave a tight smile. Not only did she have to purchase some new clothes after work, she had to spend time remaking her military ID, file a police report about her stolen purse, and find out if she'd gotten the go-ahead to start looking for off-base housing.

"It'll be fun. I promise." The doctor pressed a warm hand across Charlie's forearm.

If Demarco worried about Dr. Stern's impression of him, it would only make sense for her to take advantage of the woman's friendliness if only to annoy the special agent. Right? "Why not? Sounds like fun." Boy, would Demarco be annoyed if he found out.

Dr. Stern clapped. "Excellent. What's your number, and I'll drop you a pin for the address."

"Think I can Uber it there? I don't have a car."

Dr. Stern's mouth gaped open. "I didn't even think."

"It's okay. I've been saving since Boot Camp to buy something better than the old beater I had in grad school. Just haven't had the time."

"Let me give you a ride."

"Really?"

"Absolutely. I'm the one that invited you to go. I should be the one to help you get there."

"All right. Sounds like a plan, Dr. Stern. What time will you pick me up?"

"You're staying here on base?"

"At the motel."

"How about six fifteen? It'll take us about thirty minutes driving time. The class starts at seven. That way we have time to grab that drink I promised."

"Sure. Fine." Was this really happening? A paint-and-sip girls' night out with a scientist from work? She never imagined something like this happening when she arrived at her new assignment. Surreal.

"Add yourself as a contact." The doctor handed her cell phone to Charlie. "Let me send you a text. That'll make it easier to connect."

The young linguist typed in her number and handed the phone back.

"Perfect." The doctor stood, and as she made her way out of the conference room, she turned and said, "And call me Abigail."

Charlie sat dumbstruck in the conference room. Did that actually happen? Did Dr. Stern—no, Abigail—ask her to attend a painting class? Seemed there was a new surprise every day at A Group. What was a 'regular' work day like in the office?

———

Although the tug of the Voynich manuscript was strong, Charlie couldn't dismiss her curiosity. As she returned to her desk, she kept an eye on the window into Orr's office. Both the commander and the doctor had been talking for a while. Had Dr. Stern told them everything she knew about the evidence they'd gathered? In a world of secrets and clearances, it wasn't hard to imagine only knowing one portion of the story. Demarco and Kellerman both had provided snippets of information without context.

Maybe her outing with Dr. Stern would give her the opportunity to forge a friendship that might help her in her work life. The doctor had been interested in her translation work after all.

Sitting down at her desk and opening up the Voynich translation work in its secure and password-protected folder, Charlie held onto her own secrets. Why divulge everything she'd discovered when her A Group teammates withheld their own details?

In this world, information was power. Considering how adrift she'd felt over the last few years, to finally encounter a place where her skills were needed and her knowledge wanted, she was in no rush to give that up until she knew more.

CHAPTER 16

HOURS LATER, Charlie had made headway on her translation of both the manuscript and the pod fragments. Deep in her work, she'd managed to connect the fuller sentence structure of the manuscript to the short text pieces found in the pod.

Forward. Backward. Right. Left. Up. Down. Locked. Unlocked.

These terms were the first pod terms she uncovered.

The instructions inside the manuscript were written centuries ago. If some creature could create a pod, what was its purpose? Return to space? Did an alien land on earth and somehow manage to blend in with humans? That said a lot about the appearance of these aliens and made her rethink the strange footprints on the sand in North Dakota.

Loathe to make another embarrassing mistake in front of her peers, she weighed the idea of holding on to the information she had until she could present everything in full. Maybe she should make an appointment to meet with Commander Orr to present her findings in private.

She clicked over to her calendar to set up an appointment request for next Monday morning. That would give her the time she needed to type up something clear for a non-linguistics expert to understand. Basic English anyone could grasp. She could dumb it down. She wasn't sure the commander would believe her, so simplicity was paramount.

After selecting an available time slot on his calendar, she sent the request.

Next, she built a dictionary using a simple spreadsheet—one column for the picture of each phoneme, the transliteration of it, and the English translation. Transliteration had been a battle. The symbols had a bit of a relationship to English in her view. Could be coincidence or her own mind playing tricks on her. But she'd built an 'alphabet' of sorts and tied it to the English alphabet, which made pronunciation and reading possible.

Most of the phonemes were swirly and compared most closely to a few letters of the alphabet. She began there. What looked like an 's' or a 't' would become an 's' or a 't' in her transliteration alphabet. Most of the vowels were similar to the vowels 'o,' 'a,' and 'e.'

When she tried voicing the strange 'words' aloud, they sounded quite odd. As if they were two steps removed from a known language, yet was complete nonsense to anyone who heard it.

She whispered one particularly long and difficult 'word' as Demarco walked past her desk toward the coffee.

"I didn't notice," he said.

"Excuse me?"

He stumbled and caught himself. "I thought you asked me a question."

"What question?" She spun her chair to face him.

His gaze jumped from her to her computer screen and back again. "About the weather," he said cautiously.

She held back a laugh. "You promise you won't tell?" It wouldn't hurt to let Demarco in on a little bit of her work, would it? She'd had to keep her best discoveries to herself, just until she was solid on her findings, before sharing any of it. But maybe Demarco wouldn't spill.

He raised his eyebrows and approached her cubicle. "I'm listening."

She turned back to her computer and enlarged the spreadsheet she'd created so far. "I was trying to read some of the Voynich text." She pointed to the word he'd heard her pronounce as he'd walked by and spoke it aloud again, "Ca-low-dit-y." As she said it, she realized it could sound like 'cloudy.'

His eyes widened. "Wait, you've cracked it?" He knelt next to her chair and stared at the spreadsheet. "Did you tell the commander?"

She could let him look at a little of what she'd done. Couldn't she? "I don't know if I'd say I cracked it, but I'm able to craft my own little dictionary of sorts, and it makes it much easier to talk about the symbols if we can give voice to them. I'm trying to assign each phoneme—a little piece of text—a sound. Like our own alphabet. Makes it easier to think of the symbols as real text, as a real language."

"And the translations?" he asked. "Have you figured any of it out? What does the manuscript say? Who wrote it? Why?"

The barrage of questions surprised her. She had no idea Demarco had been so interested in the Voynich manuscript. He'd been kind to her yesterday after Orr had criticized her, but she didn't think he had real interest in the text. Who knew he almost equaled her enthusiasm? "I've been able to figure out almost all of the text from the pod. The picture where the symbols were the clearest, at least."

"Show me." He leaned in. His breath warm on her bare arm.

She shivered.

"All right." Although her intention had been to present her findings in private with Commander Orr to avoid another embarrassing outburst and ensure he was pleased with her discovery, Demarco's focused interest lifted her spirits. "I went for a swim last night, and that's when things clicked."

"You went swimming at nine o'clock at night? After I walked you back to the motel?"

"Shh." Charlie swept her gaze around the vicinity of her cubicle praying nobody else heard she and Demarco had spent time together outside work. If Stormy heard, she'd be clucking her tongue in disappointment. The office lothario and Charlie alone together? Bad news.

"Not the safest thing to do," he said in a quieter tone.

Why did she have to bristle at his concern? The chiding nature of his comment set her off. "It was perfectly safe. In fact, the commander was there."

"Was he?"

"Never mind about that. You asked about my discovery. Still interested?"

"Yes." He clasped his hands behind his back and remained kneeling next to her computer screen. "Please, I want to know more."

Clicking in her research folder, she brought up a picture of two pages in the manuscript. "The deciphering of the text inside the pods reminded me of a certain spot in the manuscript where I'd been stuck during graduate school." She pointed to a series of phonemes on the displayed pages. "This combination of phonemes didn't appear anywhere else in the manuscript. They were an isolated series of 'words' that didn't match anything else on the other pages. When I'd been doing my research and attempting a translation, these pages disrupted everything I thought I'd uncovered."

"How so?" A wrinkle appeared in the special agent's broad forehead.

How to explain to someone without her background? "Earlier, when you thought I was asking you about the weather? I was reading the Voynich 'words' using my transliteration alphabet."

He gave a quizzical look.

She clicked on the minimized spreadsheet she'd been developing. "To crack a linguistic code, you first need to separate out the phonemes. Each individual phoneme is a sound that makes up the language. For example, this one." She highlighted one of the bits of text from the manuscript. "It also appears in some of the photos we took at Devils Lake." She opened up the photos she'd categorized and labeled. "See?" She used her cursor to circle around the faded text inside the pod. "It's the same phoneme."

"Yes, I see. It's a similar chunk of script."

"Exactly." She clicked back to her spreadsheet. "I first tried to find phonemes on the photos that matched my previous work, which also helped me figure out the meaning of the words themselves. The pod 'words' were connected to travel, motion—"

"Right, you presented that idea in the All Hands meeting."

"Yes, but what I didn't have time to do before that meeting was to go back to the manuscript and see if I could find these same 'words.' And last night when I was swimming, it came to me where I had seen these pod words in the manuscript." Her heart raced, remembering the moment she'd made the connection. "These two pages. The ones I couldn't fit in with the rest of the manuscript. The two pages that eluded me, that tortured me. Why were these pages here, buried in a book mostly about plants and herbs?"

Demarco stared at her screen, the two manuscript pages maximized. "What is it? What did you find?"

She pointed out each similar word, "Here and here and here. Forward. Backward. Up. Down. Stop. Start." Her breath caught in her throat. She could hardly say the words aloud. "These are instructions for operating a machine—a machine that travels."

Demarco's face turned ashen.

Did he feel the same excitement as she? "And then when I thought about the rest of these pages in the manuscript, why the detail about so many plants?" She brought up another snapshot of two different pages in the manuscript. "It has been long surmised that the manuscript contained chemistry details. Primitive chemistry, yes, but chemistry concepts nonetheless. The pods are organic in nature. They contain no metallic or plastic or any other non-organic materials." She took a deep breath. "The Voynich Manuscript is an instruction manual for building a traveling machine. Someone in fifteenth century Italy wrote the instructions to build a pod."

Demarco brought a hand to his mouth. A pained expression marred his features.

That wasn't the reaction Charlie had been expecting. He seemed horrified by her analysis. But why?

"You're certain?" he choked out the words. "You're absolutely certain about this?"

She focused her attention on her computer screen. "That's what I've been focusing on today—when we're not being interrupted by visitors."

"I'm very sorry to have interrupted your work, Petty Officer." Dr. Stern appeared.

Charlie's face heated. The older woman had been so kind to her with her invitation, and now she'd mucked it up. "I didn't mean—it was wonderful to have you stop by and let us know what's going on with the samples we collected."

The doctor smiled broadly. "It's all right, Charlie. I can call you Charlie, can't I?" She stole a glance down the row of cubicles. "The commander can't make me use all of that formality he insists on in your office. Isn't that right, Agent Demarco?"

Charlie held back a grin at the doctor's remark.

Demarco stood and cleared his throat. "If you'll excuse me, I need to prepare for my meeting with Commander Orr."

"Of course." Dr. Stern stepped aside.

He headed toward his desk at the other end of the aisle.

"He's a mystery that one," Abigail Stern said as she watched his departure. "Warm one minute, cold the next."

"Yes." Why did he behave so oddly when she'd shared her discovery? She'd made the mistake of bringing him in on her secret only to instantly regret it. Although he'd appeared enthusiastic to learn more about her translations, his reaction had been negative. Did she put her research at risk by telling him too much too soon?

"But sometimes mysteries are fun to solve." Dr. Stern eyes shone. "I'll see you tomorrow evening, Charlie. I'm looking forward to it."

Charlie smiled and nodded, but a cold sensation invaded her gut. Demarco made her doubt, once again, trusting anyone in the office with her discoveries.

———

Charlie grabbed a red leather purse off her bed. It had been an impulse buy at the Px yesterday after work. She opened it and dropped in her brand new military ID and a wad of cash, unsure what one needed to bring to a paint-and-sip event.

Thank goodness Abigail Stern had offered to drive. After cancelling her stolen credit and bank cards, she wouldn't have had the means to pay an Uber driver. At least the Navy Credit Union on base had let her write herself a check for cash while she waited for replacement cards.

She checked her watch. Early yet. But she could wait in the lobby.

As she decided what to wear from her limited wardrobe, her brother texted her. She'd settled on a pair of jeans and a sleeveless print blouse she'd picked up on her quick shopping spree. Comfortable and casual. She slipped into some plain white running shoes, headed out the door, and read her brother's text.

> Hey, sister. Heard you're in DC. Where are you staying?

She paused in the hall and quickly answered him.

> Washington Navy Yard. The base motel. Waiting for okay to rent apt.

Three little dots appeared showing her brother was composing a response text.

Skipping down the stairs, she exited into the lobby of the motel. A tall young man with sandy blond hair stood with his back to her.

"Chad!" She'd recognize that wiry build anywhere. Opening her arms wide, she gave her slightly-younger-than-her brother a big hug.

"Surprise," he said. "Mom told me about your orders."

"It's been a whirlwind, to say the least." She stood back and gave him the once over. "Looking good, Ensign Cutter."

And he did. His face had thinned out since she saw him last—more than three years ago at his Naval Academy graduation—and the lanky body of a young man had solidified into a sturdy, muscled physique.

"It's Lieutenant JG now."

Did he blush?

"Wow." Hard to believe her brother had achieved so much in such a short period of time. His career in military intelligence was buzzing along, while hers had stalled. But she didn't begrudge him his success. He'd known what he wanted: the Navy career their father had hoped for both of them. "I didn't even realize. When?"

"Last year, when you were in Boot Camp."

She nodded. That had been a trying period in her life. She'd joined as an enlisted person without telling anyone in her family. To admit to her hard-nosed father she'd failed in graduate school had been too much to face. "I'm sorry I missed the ceremony."

"That's okay."

She pulled a face.

"No, really. It's not that big of a deal."

She rolled her eyes. "Yeah, right." She punched him in the shoulder. "Wait a minute, what are you doing in DC? I thought you'd been assigned to Rota."

Naval Station Rota in Spain provided support for U.S. and NATO ships along with Navy and Air Force flights and passengers, and also provided cargo, fuel, and ammunition to units in the region. Even some linguists were stationed there.

Her Intelligence Officer brother had received the plum assignment only a few months previous.

"I ship out in a couple of weeks. Thought I'd come see you before I got wrapped up in the move." He scanned her figure. "Looks like you have a night out planned, though."

Her stomach dropped. Why did she have to agree to Dr. Stern's invite? If only she'd known her brother would make a visit, she would've cancelled. She glanced at her watch. "My ride's going to be here in about five minutes. I'm sorry."

"Don't be worry about it. If my sister has a hot date on a Saturday night, I'm not going to get in the way."

"It's not a date."

Dr. Abigail Stern entered the lobby. "Ah, now I see why you didn't answer my text." She held up her phone. "This young fella's a lot more interesting than a boring old woman like me."

Charlie noticed the text had lit up her phone screen. "I'm sorry, Dr. Stern."

"Abigail, remember?"

"Abigail. Yes." She gestured at her brother. "I'd like you to meet my brother, Chad. He's a Lieutenant JG."

Dr. Stern nodded approvingly. "Your brother?" She squinted at them. "Yes, I can see the resemblance. Older? Younger?" She reached out and shook his hand.

"Younger," Charlie answered before her brother could open his mouth.

"By three minutes," he retorted.

"Twins. Wow." Dr. Stern studied Chad's face. "I'm kind of into DNA and the nature versus nurture argument. But I don't know if any of the remarkable similarities of identical twins—beyond shared genetics—translates to fraternal twins."

"Only if you count both of us having an allergy to strawberries," her brother said.

"I'm not sure that's really what she meant, Chad." Charlie shook her head.

"Well, it was very nice to meet you." Dr. Stern smiled and then turned to Charlie. "Shall we go then? Iris has our spots ready near the back of the class. That way we can gossip about other people's painting skills or lack thereof."

Chad raised a brow.

"We're going to a paint-and-sip thing in Fairfax." It sounded ridiculous to her own ears. When had she ever been into art?

Her brother held back a laugh. "Oh, okay." He stepped away from the two women and headed toward the door. "It was good seeing you, sis. Maybe we can find a time for dinner before I ship out."

"Absolutely." Although she'd rather spend the evening catching up with her brother, she couldn't break off her promise to the doctor.

"Excellent." He gave her a double thumbs up.

She longingly watched Chad walk out into the parking lot.

Abigail Stern linked arms with Charlie. "Let's go have some fun, shall we?"

Charlie plastered on a smile and decided to make the best of it. If nothing else, she could build up a rapport with someone important to her career, and that was worth it...wasn't it?

CHAPTER 17

DR. ABIGAIL STERN drove a late model BMW X3. As they headed down 395 south across the Potomac toward Fairfax, the interior of the luxury SUV remained whisper quiet. Charlie stroked the soft brown leather seats absentmindedly. Quite a difference from the variety of low-end used vehicles she'd driven since high school.

"Do you and your brother get along?" Dr. Stern asked.

"We're pretty close." A twin, even a fraternal one, had a relationship difficult to describe to outsiders. "My mom claims we had a secret language when we were little."

Dr. Stern turned on her blinker and expertly changed lanes to miss a traffic slowdown. "Fascinating."

"Honestly, I think we were toddlers babbling nonsense. I don't remember any of it." The memory of a proud mother exclaiming her children's brilliance to another mother at a school event flashed in her mind. "But I do enjoy languages, so who knows?"

"Both you and your brother ended up in the military, how did that come about?"

Charlie let out a breath, glanced out the window at the jam

of cars, and carefully answered, "My dad is in the Navy, too. Sort of a family tradition, I guess." Her stomach tightened. Why did she feel irritable every time the topic of her father came up?

"The Navy sent you to school to learn linguistics?" the doctor asked.

"No." If only Dr. Stern knew how much she'd tried to avoid a military career. "I had other plans before I joined the Navy."

"I see. That's not uncommon." She applied the brake, checked her mirrors, and maneuvered around an old panel van that refused to keep up with the flow of cars on the highway. "Some of us take time to find what our gifts are and how best to use them."

Charlie nodded. But the way her current job lined up perfectly with her deep interest in the manuscript, she believed more in fate than choices made. "How did you end up on the team?"

"Commander Orr and I go back a ways."

"Oh?" The more she learned about NCIS-A, the more surprises she uncovered.

"We've both had an interest in astrobiology. We met at a Department of Defense conference years ago in Las Vegas. I was a guest speaker in a symposium about Unidentified Objects and the possibility of life in outer space. David— Commander Orr—introduced himself afterwards. His father had been involved in some sort of project." She tapped her fingers on the steering wheel. "What was it called? I can't remember now. He was quite vague, considering we were in an open forum."

Charlie understood the need for secrecy. "His father was also military?"

"Yes, some higher up muckety-muck. He was killed in a

military exercise out in the desert just as David was graduating from the Naval Academy. A real tragedy."

"How awful." Charlie's perspective of her new boss changed with that piece of information. As much as she and her father clashed, she couldn't imagine him no longer in her life.

"I had a feeling his deep connection to alien theory was related to his father's unexpected passing. He asked me all kinds of questions about remnants of meteorites and some reports about alien bacteria found by the astronauts on the International Space Station. We had a very pleasant lunch, and I gave him my card. Who knew years later, he would contact me about joining his team?"

"The commander seems to be able to track down almost anyone."

Abigail Stern laughed. "True." She took the turn off to 495 at Springfield and changed topics. "Thanks again for agreeing to come with me. It really means a lot to my cousin."

"Of course." Charlie listed things in her mind she'd rather be doing on a Saturday night: streaming a movie, doing laundry, polishing her shoes. "I'm sure it will be fun." Did she sound convincing?

"Joyce divorced a few years ago and had to start over. She'd been a stay-at-home mom for a long time. Hadn't worked since before her kids. She was an art teacher and always thought she'd go back to it, but never did."

"I'm sorry to hear that."

"About the divorce?" the doctor asked. "She couldn't be happier, really. She plowed her half of their home equity into the paint-and-sip and has loved every second of it."

"Well, I hope she's good at teaching. I'm hopeless when it comes to artistic talents."

"You've seen the paintings in my lab, right?" Dr. Stern burst into laughter.

Charlie couldn't help but join in. "I didn't want to be insulting—"

The response drove the middle-aged woman to snort in between laughs. "Honey, it'd be very hard to insult me. Trust me, you're in good hands with Joyce."

———

Fifteen minutes later, the two women pulled up in front of a well-lit two-story building with apartments for rent above and businesses below. A sign above one of the storefronts read "Some Enchanted Painting."

Cute.

Dr. Stern completed a perfect parallel parking job, clapped her hands together and said, "Let's order that first glass, shall we? I think I owe you."

Any signs of a serious scientist had disappeared on the drive from DC to Fairfax. Who knew Charlie could have such a lovely night out with a colleague? "I think I'll have a shiraz."

"Excellent choice. I'm more of a white wine drinker myself."

They entered the studio together and were the first to arrive.

A tall, elegant woman with a gorgeous riot of black curly hair and wearing a paint-splattered white smock greeted them with a smile. "Abby, you made it." She enveloped her cousin in a hug. "And you brought a friend." She touched Charlie on the shoulder and squeezed. "I'm Joyce. Welcome. I reserved Abby's favorite spot in the back."

"This is Charlie Cutter. She's a new co-worker."

"How nice." Joyce led them to the last row of tables, which

stood closest to the floor-to-ceiling window that faced the side-walk. "You can put your things here and then we can chat over a glass while we wait for the rest of the students."

Charlie set her red purse next to a table-sized easel that held an empty canvas. Two brushes, a cup of water, a blank palette, and a few paper towels lay on the table in front of the easel.

The three women made their way to the back of the studio. Dozens of paintings lined the walls from waist-high to the ceiling—animals, landscapes, fantasy worlds, farms, city views.

Charlie recognized a few that she'd seen in Dr. Stern's lab. "Where do you come up with all of your ideas? This is amazing."

Joyce slipped behind the small bar in one corner and set three glasses on the counter. "Some I come up with on my own. Others are ideas I find on the internet." She shrugged. "I know Abby wants a white. What's your preference, Charlie?"

"A shiraz?" Charlie scanned the bottles lining the wall on a cabinet behind Joyce.

"Absolutely." Joyce picked up a bottle and poured. "This one's from Australia."

The door jingled.

"I'll be right with you," Joyce greeted the newly arrived students and finished filling Charlie's glass. "Guess we'll have to have that chat later. Excuse me."

Joyce headed to the front of the studio to engage with her customers.

Dr. Stern turned to take a gander at who would be in their class for the evening. "Well, this is a surprise." She nudged Charlie. "Angel, when did he become interested in art?"

Charlie choked on her first sip of wine. It couldn't be.

· · ·

Angel Demarco ushered a beautiful brunette into the studio. When he caught sight of Charlie, his smile wavered. "Cutter?"

Joyce raised a brow, "You all know each other?"

Dr. Stern stepped forward and reached out a hand, "Angel is also part of our team, but I don't believe I've met you, miss—?"

Demarco's date accepted the hand shake. "You can call me Clarissa." She spoke with a honeyed Southern accent and wore a slinky blue dress more suited to a nightclub than a painting class.

"Wonderful. I'm Abigail, and this is Charlie." The doctor grabbed Charlie by the elbow and drew her forward.

The shiraz in her glass threatened to slosh over the rim. "Hello." She waved and knew her smile probably appeared fake because it felt fake.

Demarco's mouth turned down. "I didn't realize you would be here."

"And I'm surprised to see you here," said the doctor. "You'd made it clear a while ago that my art didn't interest you."

Did he turn red? His ears certainly did.

"Angel told me he couldn't wait for our date and said he was going to take me some place special," Clarissa gushed and clutched his bicep. "I wasn't quite expecting this." She gestured at the art-strewn walls. "I don't think he knew how much I've always wanted to do one of these silly little classes."

Joyce's eyes widened at the slight. "Let me show you where you'll be sitting. My assistant will be here in a minute to serve you your drinks." With incredible grace, Joyce showed her customers to their seats.

Dr. Stern excused herself to use the ladies' room.

Clarissa claimed a seat in the front row near the middle. Joyce handed her a utilitarian smock, and the elegantly dressed woman appeared at a loss.

As Joyce helped her don the smock to protect her clothing, Demarco took the opportunity to speak to Charlie. "What are you doing here?"

"Dr. Stern invited me." Charlie took a sip of her wine. "What are you doing here?" she lobbed back at him. Why did Clarissa's appearance annoy her so?

His mouth set in a line. "Excuse me, but I'd like to go back to my date." He left Charlie standing in the aisle.

Although he'd avoided answering her question, she had an inkling why Demarco might've shown up, and her name was Abigail Stern. He'd do almost anything to win her over. The thought of it made her hold back a laugh. He had no interest in painting. Dr. Stern knew it, and now he was stuck here with his date for the next two hours.

Dr, Stern retrieved her wine glass from the bar and rejoined Charlie. "We might as well take our seats. Class is going to start in a little bit. Not sure how many other students are signed up, but yesterday I'd only seen two registered, and I guess we know who made that reservation."

Charlie snickered.

Dr. Stern shook her head. "He's been acting this way ever since the screw up last year."

"The lost evidence?"

They took their seats at the back of the classroom.

"Yes. He'd only been with the team for a few months, and we had no security procedures in place for our specific circumstances." Dr. Stern tied on her smock. "He still thinks I blame him for the loss."

"Do you?"

The door opened, interrupting their conversation.

"Welcome," Joyce said, greeting the next couple who entered. "I'm Joyce, and I'll be your teacher this evening."

———

An hour into the class, Charlie admitted defeat. "I give up." Why did her owl look more like a chicken? She didn't have a light touch for the finer details or maybe the second glass of shiraz had something to do with it.

"It's not so bad." The doctor, who Charlie had gotten more comfortable calling Abigail, consoled her. "I'll have to show you some of my first paintings. Atrocious." She switched her gaze to Demarco and his date. "I think Angel created a crime scene on his canvas."

Charlie held back a laugh. "Think he'll hang it in the office?"

"I'll bet you a dollar he doesn't."

"That's a bet I won't take." It was easier to make jokes about Demarco then to deal with her feelings. Every time he leaned his head toward Clarissa or touched her arm or her leg, an uncomfortable burn built in her chest.

As Joyce moved to the next step in the instructions, the two women dabbed and daubed, attempting to recreate the example.

At the exact same moment, two cell phones in the studio chimed.

Charlie thrust her hand into her purse.

Demarco pulled his flip phone out of his pants pocket.

She read the text that popped up in their encrypted messaging app.

> ALERT: Radar signature detected.
> Coordinates to follow.

Her pulse quickened. Another pod.

"Abigail, I'm so sorry, but I have to go." She untied the smock and then touched the Uber app on her phone.

"Come on, Cutter. Let's go." Demarco already stood by the door. "I can give you a ride."

His date, in shock, sat frozen with her mouth open and a paintbrush in her hand.

CHAPTER 18

"THE COORDINATES ARE COMING IN." Charlie gripped her new iPhone and stared at the three dots in the text chat.

"Doesn't make much of a difference. We need to get back to HQ." Demarco turned onto the 495 on-ramp headed his vintage Landcruiser back to DC. "Hope you put your go-bag together. Mine's in the trunk."

Her thoughts fluttered to her cramped motel room and the pile of new clothes stacked on her bed. "It'll take me five minutes. I swear."

"That's what every woman says," he mumbled.

"Hold on. They sent a pin." She pressed on the link in the message. "I'd at least like to know if I need to grab my passport."

"You don't keep it in that red monstrosity?" He gestured at the purse in her lap. "You could fit a small horse in there."

The map appeared.

What were the odds?

"We don't need to go to the meet-up location." Her nerve endings tingled.

"What are you talking about?" As they approached a highway sign, he pointed. "This is our exit. 395."

"The pod. It landed not too far from us." She expanded her map with her two fingers. "Near Colchester. In the Occoquan River."

"Shit." Instantly, his demeanor changed. "I need to take you back to Dr. Stern."

"What?" Her mouth dropped open. "A pod is about to land. Are you crazy?"

They neared the exit.

"I'm the security expert. It's too dangerous for you."

How dare he imply she couldn't handle the risks involved with her job.

"Screw that." She held up the map so he could see the pin location. "Switch lanes." She pointed at his last opportunity to merge onto the correct exit ramp heading south.

The special agent glanced at the map. "Dammit, Cutter."

He poured on the gas, and the 1970s gas guzzler picked up speed. The Prius next to him in the correct exit lane refused to move. Laying on the horn, Demarco sped up. An opportunity to squeeze in front of the electric vehicle was closing quickly. The separate exit lanes split in fifty yards. Orange barrels filled the triangle between them.

"You have to move over." Charlie checked over her shoulder. "Maybe if you slow down—"

"I'm not fucking slowing down."

The engine throttled. He leaned forward. The Prius matched him in speed. He met the gaze of the young woman driver with short green hair and a pair of purple-rimmed glasses.

"If you don't slow down, we're going to crash." Charlie braced herself. Would the seatbelts in this old thing work?

The lanes split. They rushed toward the orange barrels.

Charlie held her breath.

Demarco milked a little more speed out of the Land-cruiser. He turned the wheel and slid the vehicle right between the surprised Prius owner and the oblivious Ford Focus ahead.

"Hell yes!" He slammed his hand on the dash. "I knew this baby wouldn't let me down."

Her nerves jangled. She hid her trembling, empty hand under her thigh and tightly clenched her phone with the other. "Can we please reach the coordinates in one piece?"

He breathed heavily for a few seconds. "If I let you come with me—"

"If? What are you going to do? Drop me off on a dark street corner and hope an Uber finds me before I get mugged?" He was unbelievable. "We're part of a team. I can't believe you are even suggesting such a thing."

He gripped the steering wheel more tightly. "I swear, Cutter, sometimes you make me want to throttle you."

"Why? Because I question your decisions? Demand to be treated with respect?"

"I'm only trying to keep you safe," he spat out.

"Safe from what? The aliens? The pods?" If they weren't traveling seventy miles an hour down the highway, she'd slap him. "I'm here because Commander Orr wanted me on the team. He thought I could handle it—why don't you?"

Demarco's phone rang and cut through the tension. "Hey, Commander Orr. I'm about—" He snapped his fingers to get her attention and pointed at her phone.

Unbelievable.

She held up the map.

He smiled. "—thirty minutes out from the location. Meet you there."

He snapped the phone shut.

Her annoyance boiled over. "You will not be dropping me off anywhere."

"Fine." He kept his eyes on the road.

"Good."

"But you will follow orders."

"I'm not your subordinate."

He talked over her protest, "Until I can ensure the site is secure."

She crossed her arms. "Let's just get there."

The sun had set, and the only view she had was the headlights from the opposite lane.

"That's what I'm trying to do," he said.

"And I'm trying to do my job, too."

He sighed. "Let's meet in the middle, jettison the feelings, and be professional."

"That's all I ever wanted." Maybe one of these days he'd overcome whatever problem he had with her. Would he treat Stormy like this?

He let a few beats pass. "Think the doc will drive Clarissa home?"

An image of the attractive brunette popped into her head. "Why wouldn't she?"

"I don't know." He ran a hand through his short hair. "That woman hates me."

"Dr. Stern doesn't hate you."

"You only met her a few days ago," he said changing lanes to follow the faster traffic. "How would you know?"

"She's been nothing but kind to me."

"Exactly." He emphasized his declaration with a pointed finger. "I knew she'd like you."

"Why do you say that?" She studied the map.

He glanced at her quickly before directing his gaze at the highway. "You're smart, driven, educated."

Her cheeks heated at his description.

"You're a lot like her."

How did he expect her to respond? One minute he found her irritating, the next minute he tossed out compliments.

He sighed. "What exit am I looking for?"

"One sixty one." She followed the route further south. "Then we'll be on Route 1. We need to find Frenchman's Point, where the river feeds into Belmont Bay."

"Deeper water?"

"Could be."

Deeper water meant the pod could disintegrate within minutes, and all opportunities to collect samples—or encounter a passenger—would be lost.

"Does this thing go any faster?" She glanced at his speedometer.

Demarco pressed the gas pedal to the floor. "We're going to find out."

————

The streets had narrowed quickly after they'd left the main road. Modest homes on several acres dotted the area. Demarco slowed the Landcruiser to a crawl. "Are you sure we're going the right way?"

"Turn here. Bell Avenue. It goes right to the water."

After he made the turn, the woods surrounded them on all sides. Not a house in sight.

"Maybe that's why no one called anything in," Charlie said.

She'd been texting with the group and giving them regular updates on their location to the object. Stormy, camping near

Deep Creek Lake with her family for the weekend, had been given the task of monitoring the news and social media sites for any unusual reports. So far, so good. It would take her two hours longer than everyone else to reach the location of the pod.

"Dead end." Demarco parked on the shoulder.

Only a single large mansion sat at the end of the road. The place appeared abandoned. No lights. No vehicles in the long semi-circular driveway.

She opened the passenger door. "Summer home?" The dead silence chilled her.

"Maybe." Demarco climbed out and opened the trunk.

A warm wind blew through the trees, and branches rubbed together. Charlie shook off an unsettling feeling.

"Cutter, get back in the rig." He closed the lid of trunk and tucked a gun in his waistband.

She stepped back. "Whoa, is that necessary?"

"Security, remember?" He opened the passenger side door for her. "You stay here. I'm going to do a perimeter check."

The last time she held a gun, she'd been in Boot Camp and a bundle of nerves. "I don't like this."

"Didn't we agree to meet in the middle?" he reminded her. "I'm going first. Once I make sure everything is safe, I'll give you a signal."

"What kind of signal?" Reluctantly, she reclaimed her seat inside the Toyota.

"Three flashes." He showed her using the Maglite he held. "Like this."

Demarco headed toward the driveway. "Don't move until I give the signal."

Charlie sank in her seat. The special agent crept toward the house and the blackness beyond. Her stomach didn't appreciate the stress as it flip-flopped with every twitch of a branch, every unidentified shadow.

———

Five long minutes later, no signal from Demarco. The hair rose on the back of her neck. Where was he? Did she miss his signal?

She scanned from the house to her left all the way across the side yard to her right, which led to the Occoquan River. Although it was a clear night, the moon hadn't yet risen in the sky. A few lights across the river winked on—other large mansions who shared the same stretch of water.

Then, in the opposite direction Demarco had headed, Charlie spied a strange green glow in the middle of the river. The weird light drew her gaze, and she fixated on the spot. Did any of the pod reports indicate a light had been seen?

As her eyes grew accustomed to the dark, the green glow revealed the curve of a sphere, half-sunk in the deep water between the mansion at the end of Bell Avenue and the lighted mansion on the opposite shore.

The pod!

It could slip beneath the water at any moment.

She burst out of the vehicle and headed toward the shore. Stupid Demarco and his 'security' crap might very well leave an alien being to drown. Why in the hell did he think a gun was necessary?

The mansion had been built on a rocky, unforgiving stretch of beach. A deck ran the length of the back of the house with a wide set of steps that led to a rather ugly water line. A rotting dock about twenty feet in length slumped in the Occoquan River—perhaps a leftover from the house that stood here before the mansion had been built.

To the east of the rotting dock a series of brand new posts had been embedded in the river bottom. A floating crane was tied up next to them. In a few days a brand new dock would be in place. Maybe the mansion wasn't empty after all.

Charlie glanced over her shoulder to ensure none of the lights were on inside the large home and to make one last attempt to spy Demarco. Where the hell was he?

Well beyond the rotting dock and the brand new posts, the eerie glow lit up the dark water at the mouth of the bay. It emanated from a single spot and flickered as the water sloshed against the now visible soft green exterior.

Charlie kicked off her running shoes.

No way was an alien going to die on her watch. Security or not.

"Hey, Cutter, what do you think you're doing?" Demarco called from the deck of the mansion.

"I'm going to swim for it," she yelled back.

She shimmied out of her jeans, and the cool evening air hit her bare legs. If he wasn't going to do anything, she would. "This might be our only chance to see who's inside. An alien species. I have to save him." She picked her way to the water.

"Wait!" His voice came from deep in his chest. "Don't!"

Warning? Or fearful?

"I can make it." She eyed the distance a second time. A few lengths of the pool at most.

"It's too dangerous. Stop!"

The greenish glow flickered.

"We don't have much time," she whispered.

Before Demarco could stop her, she walked into the river up to her waist. Ahead, in the dark, the flickering glow called to her. Inside, she imagined a foreign creature, perhaps millions of lightyears away from its home, struggling to survive.

With strong strokes she swam toward the pod. Distantly, she could hear Demarco yelling something at her. His words were lost to the breeze and the sound of the water lapping against her body. As her legs kicked and her arms fell into a rhythm, her mind turned to the pages of the Voynich manuscript, the strange writing, the formula to build a pod, and the many questions she had for this traveler.

Her fingers touched a softness. Abruptly, she lifted her face from the water. An eight-foot-wide pod bobbed in the river, its hull gooey and with a dent in its top. The glow grew fainter. How much time did she have left before it sank beneath the surface?

She paddled around the object searching for a way in. A door. A hatch. Even a crack. She encountered nothing but green mushy smoothness.

From within she heard a muffled cry. A long sad wail.

It tore at her heart.

An alien arrived to earth only to choke to death in foreign waters.

"Hello?" she called out. "I'm here. How do I get in?" Although she knew the alien couldn't possibly understand her words, she wanted the creature to know he wasn't alone.

The crying stopped.

"Mama?" a little voice said.

Slowly, a hatched opened. Water rushed in.

Charlie swam toward it, unafraid at what she might encounter. Driven by pity and an odd lightness of being, she reached the hatch.

A small creature, three feet in height, dressed crudely in a tunic made of a rough material stood before her. He lost his footing as the pod dipped further under the surface of the river.

"Mama," he said again. "Mama."

The creature leapt into the water and clung to her. Unable to paddle with both arms, Charlie fought to keep her head above water with a forceful tread of her legs.

And it was then Charlie realized she had not rescued an alien being. She'd rescued a little boy.

THE END

Continued in Decryption, Book 2 in The Genesis Machine Trilogy

Join K.J. Gillenwater's newsletter and receive a free science fiction short story

DECRYPTION
THE GENESIS MACHINE, BOOK 2

1498. Val Camonica, Northern Italy.

Risa squeezed her son's hand. Crouching in the bushes on the edge of the woods in the dark would frighten any little boy. Being chased by a fearful mob multiplied that feeling times ten, times one hundred.

One times ten is ten.

Two times ten is twenty.

Three times ten is thirty.

Her mind latched on to the things that comforted her: numbers, logic, science.

Things a woman shouldn't know.

Things a woman could get killed for.

Things that not only she could be killed for, but her child. Her innocent child. It was as if an invisible hand squeezed her heart.

She could not lose her child to this mob of witch hunters.

Voices shouted nearby. Lantern light shot through the dark. Dozens of lanterns.

They'd never make it.

How much further to go?

Pushing through the shrubs, she dragged her exhausted child with her.

"Mama," he wailed.

She clamped a hand over his mouth. "*Tranquillo*, little one." She knelt on the soft grass and gathered him in her arms. "We are almost there. I need you to be very brave for me. Can you do that?"

The boy nodded and clutched her tightly around the neck. "*Ho paura*, mama."

She whispered into his blond hair, "I know, *caro*." She stood and held his hand tightly. "Come, we're almost there, and then we'll be safe. I promise. *Promesso*."

But she didn't know if her promise would come to fruition. She'd only finished crafting the machines in the last few days. The first one had been an abject failure. It had turned into a pile of green mush within moments. The formula not quite the same as she'd remembered.

Her experiments had caught the notice of the wrong people. Not the friendly nuns who'd taken her in--a lost, pregnant woman with no husband. But the religious fanatics who increasingly feared the dark arts and blamed innocent women as the perpetrators. In the last year, their fears reached a fever pitch, and focus turned toward the *donna strana* at the nunnery.

Who was she? Where had she come from? Why did she speak a foreign tongue? Why was she seen late at night in the woods near the river? Was her child a child of the devil?

Although the nuns had welcomed her into their nunnery years ago, they'd questioned her strange clothing and mysterious arrival. But when they'd learned of her ability to read and write, they'd found her quite useful.

So they had given her sanctuary despite the suspicions of those outside the cloister. A very much needed sanctuary. For within her mind, resided the secret to returning to her life and the father of her child.

"*Lei è andata così!*" one of her accusers bellowed.

They were mere steps behind her and her son. The pounding of her heart filled her ears until she could hear nothing else. Branches scratched at her face and tore at her rough woolen dress and the kirtle underneath.

Ahead she saw the machines, lurking in a copse of trees in order to blend in with their green leaves. She dropped her son's hand, leaving him in a marshy meadow dotted with moonlight, and raced toward them. In the spongy hull she pressed a hidden button to expose a hatch.

"Come, *caro*, come. You must get inside." Risa beckoned her child forward.

The rumble of the mob crashing through the woods made her breath hitch in her throat. She'd seen what they'd done to others accused of being witches: torture, burning, horrible things. But a child? What would they do to an innocent child? The horror too much for her mind.

"*Non voglio,*" he said, planting his feet in the soft meadow grasses. "No."

There was no time to waste. No time to cajole. Her voice grew sharp, and she hated herself for it. "Get inside. *Ora!*" She grabbed him by the arm and dragged him into the machine.

He was afraid of the dark, and the machine appeared to be a black hole.

"No, mama! No!" Her son fought against her.

"Sit." She shoved him into the single seat inside the machine and strapped him in. The flexible restraint melded with it as if it had always been a part of it.

"Mama!" The boy cried and struggled in the tight restraint.

She wished she'd had time to explain to him what was happening, where he was going, and why. Risa thought she would have had more time. In fact, she wasn't even sure the machines would function properly. The original machine she'd arrived in had failed miserably. She was so far off course and had no idea why. A fault of design? A bad program?

"*Eccola!*" the mob entered into the meadow. "*E anche il suo bambino diavolo!*"

"Lord help us," she whispered. She'd never let them take her son. Never.

She fiddled with the controls and set it as best she could remember. It had been years since she'd been inside a machine. Would Byron be on the other side waiting for him? Would someone make sure he was reunited with his father?

No time to waste. She had no choice. She entered the last of the data.

"I will see you there. Do not fear." She touched his tear-stained cheek and then kissed him on the forehead. "*Ti amo figlio mio.*"

Rough hands pulled her out of the machine.

The boy cried and struggled in the seat. "Mama!"

"My son!" she cried in an agonized voice. These animals might kill her, but they would not touch her child.

She raged against the arms that held her. Stinking, dirty, soulless humans. The same kind of men who'd destroyed her world. The same kind of men who'd forced her to flee for her life and her child's life once before. She screamed and bit at her captors' hands. Flailing like a wild cat, she broke free and lunged for the shell of the machine. The meat of her palm pressed the hidden button a second time.

As the hatch closed, a wave of relief filled her. He would be safe. No matter what happened to her, he would be safe.

A heavy object landed with a crack on her skull. Warm blood poured out and ran down her face. It was too late. The other machine would remain unused and disintegrate in the next heavy downpour. But as she lost consciousness and fell into the arms of the men who surrounded her, she smiled as the machine began to spin and spin and spin. Faster and faster until it turned into a blur of motion and green.

"My son," she whispered one last time.

The machine disappeared, and the men fell back in fear.

Continue reading the next book in The Genesis Machine trilogy, Decryption.

ABOUT THE AUTHOR

K. J. Gillenwater has a B.A. in English and Spanish from Valparaiso University and an M.A. in Latin American Studies from University of California, Santa Barbara. She worked as a Russian linguist in the U.S. Navy, spending time at the National Security Agency doing secret things. After six years of service, she ended up as a technical writer in the software industry. She has lived all over the U.S. and currently resides in Wyoming with her family where she runs her own business writing government proposals and squeezes in fiction writing when she can. In the winter she likes to ski and snowshoe; in the summer she likes to garden with her husband and take walks with her dog.

Visit K.J.'s website for more information about her writing, her books, and what's coming next. www.kjgillenwater.com.

If you enjoyed this book, K. J. Gillenwater is the author of multiple books, which are available in print and in eBook format at multiple vendors.

- The Genesis Machine Trilogy: Inception, Decryption, and Revelation
- Revenge Honeymoon
- Illegal
- Aurora's Gold
- The Ninth Curse

- The Little Black Box
- Acapulco Nights
- Blood Moon

Short Stories & Short Story Collections:

- Skyfall
- Nemesis
- The Man in 14C
- Charlie and the Zombie Factory

Made in the USA
Columbia, SC
11 January 2024

30293124R00121